The Haunting of Pear Tree Cottage

Debbie Chase

This is a work of fiction. Names, characters, places, and incidents are products of the author's imagination or are used fictitiously and are not to be construed as real. Any resemblance to actual events, locations, organizations, or persons, living or dead, is entirely coincidental.

World Castle Publishing, LLC
Pensacola, Florida

Paperback ISBN: 9781956788266
eBook ISBN: 9781956788273
First Edition World Castle Publishing, LLC, December 6, 2021
http://www.worldcastlepublishing.com

Cover: Karen Fuller
Editor: Maxine Bringenberg

Chapter One

The house looked different from when I saw it for the first time just a few months before, its appearance now dark and empty, and its windows like creepy blind eyes. The scrubby grass in the pocket-sized garden was infested with weeds, mainly dandelions shining bright yellow. All the flowers had died back into the earth and, because of autumn, leaves of blazing orange, red, and crimson skittered and twisted into crispy piles on the ground. I hoisted the first of many suitcases from the boot of my car and, pushing open the gate with a foot, trundled it noisily up the garden path.

I noticed the name of the house, "Pear Tree Cottage," the letters old now and faded, the sign coming loose from the wall. Glancing at the garden, I wondered where the pear tree was. There didn't seem to be one now, but surely there would have been many years before. A face appeared fleetingly at next door's window, making me jump, a pale oval that stared hard with narrowed eyes as, with a shaking hand, I fished the key from my pocket and unlocked the door.

Stepping into the hallway, a fetid musty smell hit me mingled with a sooty odor, totally at odds with the fresh salty breeze that blew outside from the tumbling Whitby Sea. Panic gripped me hard, like a hand around my throat, as I realized how far away I was from Leeming in West Yorkshire, the village where I was born and where I'd lived until now, for the first twenty-eight years of my life.

The estate agent, Mr. Bright, had gone over and above by lighting a fire in the sitting room's beautiful cast iron fireplace, which was still smoldering bright red, yet the rest of the house felt cold. I found the boiler hidden in a cupboard in the long narrow galley kitchen, which sprung to life at the touch of a button, orange light glowing, a comforting hum keeping me company in the oppressive silence of the house. Peering from the window, I saw a small yard at the back surrounded by a high brick wall, empty but for the bins lined up in a row—green, brown, and blue.

Keeping my long leather coat wrapped firmly around me, I wandered from room to room, taking it all in, planning what I would put in each one. The bedroom was cozy and had built-in wardrobes occupying one whole side, with cream painted doors and deep latches. The ceiling was low and crisscrossed with thick dark beams, and the walls were rough and misshapen as a bag of broken biscuits.

I stood at the window, the radiator warm now through my jeans, and looked down onto the front garden, the brown of the path zigzagging crazily through the green of the tufty grass. Looking straight ahead over the pitched roofs of neighboring houses, the thin brown line of the sea and the sand were clearly visible, and a tang of salt, inching in through the ill-fitting window filled the room like a fog. The filmy white shapes of seagulls fluttered in the sky, their plaintive cries both sad and eerie, sending shivers running down my spine.

Downstairs I noticed a mirror hanging over the fireplace, a pretty one, oval-shaped with a thin gold band etched around the edge. Obviously, it must have belonged to the lady who lived here before. I gazed at myself, noticing that my face, almost devoid of makeup, just a slick of lipstick and smudged eyeliner, looked tired, and there were deep black pouches like shopping bags beneath my eyes. If only this was Snow White's mirror, and it could turn me into a beauty.

A sudden movement caught my eye, and I saw something black in the corner of the mirror, something that had a face, a blurry face I could barely see—something that was staring at me. My heart pounding away in my breast, tentatively, I put out a finger to rub it away as if it was just a grubby mark, but I pulled back, scared of what I might touch. I looked over my shoulder, but there was nothing there, yet the air felt cold and clammy, and a chill ran through me. My hand shaking, I flicked on the overhead light and did a tour of the room, checking carefully in the corners, looking for a black hooded figure, but there was definitely nothing there. I took another sneaky peek in the glass, my heart pounding hard, but there was nothing. It was gone.

I laughed to myself, thinking it must be my imagination or stress, perhaps. I'd moved here today to this lovely little terraced cottage in Whitby, which was old—well, ancient really—and brimming with history. Speaking of history, I'd come all the way from West Yorkshire, a little village called Leeming in Oxenhope, which had two historic claims to fame. The first being that it was close to Haworth, the home of the Bronte sisters and their books, *Jane Eyre*, and *Wuthering Heights* and many more. The other claim to fame? The pretty little train station at Oakworth, a stone's throw from Haworth, the name of the station "Oakworth" spelled out in white stones on the grass—and the classic film, *The Railway Children*.

From the window of the rented house I'd shared with my boyfriend, Stuart, I'd been able to see the reservoir at Leeming. I loved to watch sparks of yellow sunshine glinting on its flat mirrored surface and see the water as it froze and floated in clumps like tiny icebergs amongst the swans, ducks, and irritable honking geese. We used to climb the rutted stony paths to the Dog & Gun Inn or walk to Oxenhope Village, where we'd sit in the park and eat fish and chips laced with salt and vinegar and wrapped in rustling paper.

Stuart and I had had six more or less happy years before Anna came on the scene. Tall, willowy Anna, who beguiled him with her long black hair and eyes dark and glistening as sloes. She was so unlike me. Where she was so dark, I was short and curvy with blue eyes, and my hair was blonde and hung loose to my shoulders, curly as a cherub's. Stuart's hair was dark too, with dark eyes just like hers, and he had a natural year round tan from working outside on his mum and dad's farm.

There was barely enough time for my side of the bed to cool before she moved in and took my place. I'd had to go back to my childhood home with my mum, who, while generally quite supportive, allowed me to stay purely, I think, for the rent she knew I could afford from my job as a legal PA in a solicitor's office in Keighley. I tried, I really did, to carry on living in Leeming, but it was so hard bumping into Stuart and Anna and watching them doing exactly the same things he and I used to do. Needless to say, men were now a thing of the past. It doesn't matter who it might be. It could be, I don't know—Lenny Kravitz! He could come and live next door, and I wouldn't bat an eyelid.

At a very low ebb and not knowing what to do, call it providence or fate, but one miserable weekend wasting time in the local library idly flicking through a national newspaper, I saw the job that was to become mine. It was a tiny advert, just a square in the corner of the page, an advert I almost missed. Wigglesworth & Horner, a firm of solicitors in Whitby, were looking for a legal PA.

Whitby brought back happy childhood memories of sunny seaside holidays, building sandcastles on the sandy beach, and swimming in the sea. I was sure I could settle there. And then, another quirk of fate—the house. The house that is now mine, situated in, would you believe it, Whitby. The house that was going cheap because it needed modernization and had been standing empty for such a long time. The house that was owned by our next door neighbor's aunt, who had moved all the way up to Scotland. Everything fell into place, the job and the house as if it was all meant to be.

And so here I was with a whole week before I started my new job. A whole week to set my new house in order and acquaint myself with Whitby. The kettle had been found and the coffee brewed, strong and thick and black, the odor wreathing around the rooms like smoke, transforming the house into a home—my home.

~*~

I awoke with a start, my heart chugging along like a steam train pulling in at Oakworth station. The duvet had slithered away and was lying on the floor, a ghostly white mound in the darkened bedroom. Grabbing hold of it, I hoisted it back up and wrapped it around my shivering body as, gradually, my eyes became accustomed to the dim. A sudden bright light fell through the un-curtained window, blinding as an eighty-watt bulb, and the great globe of the moon swam into view, staring in at me with its cold blank face.

Tiny pattering footsteps sounded on the stone stairs, making the hairs rise on the back of my neck. I couldn't move—I could barely breathe. I was paralyzed except for my heart beating fast as a pulse right up into my throat. Was this house haunted? My mind went back to the black shape I thought I'd seen in the mirror, the hooded apparition I was so sure had been there, and the chill in the sitting room even though the fire was blazing and the central heating on. Had it scared me more than I cared to admit and paved the way for this ghostly experience?

The moon disappeared from the window, throwing the room into darkness as slowly, cautiously, clutching the duvet around me for protection, I got up from the bed and, going to the door, put my ear close and listened. All I could hear at first was my own panicked breathing. But then came a tiny scratching like mice or rats, a little cry like a mew, and a pattering like fingernails against the other side of the door. My hand shaking, I carefully lifted the latch and slowly drew the door open, not knowing what to expect, dreading what would come through the gaping dark hole of the doorway.

A black shape flew into the room, hissing and spitting and running in demented circles. It seemed to bounce around the walls as if it were flying, claws outstretched. I ducked my arms over my head. Oh my God! Was it a bat? Was it Dracula? The moon showed its eerie blank face again, lighting up the room so I could see what this hideous creature was. And, it was a cat! A cat? I moved nearer to the black fluffy creature. It didn't move, didn't even back away, but just looked at me nonchalantly with eyes that shone bright as orange topaz. It leapt like a mini athlete onto the bed and began to wash itself casually with its tiny rough tongue.

"Who are you?" I asked, backing away slightly and pulling the duvet closer to my body. "How did you get in?"

"Meow," it replied and then carried on washing, its tongue very pink amongst the black fur, moving its head from side to side, so I caught a glint of silver. Hanging from its red collar was a name tag. *Moses,* it said on the little silver disc. That's all. Just its name, Moses. Hadn't Mum's neighbor said that her aunt had a cat she was taking with her? Had Moses travelled all the way from Scotland to come back home?

I peered at the disc again but could see no phone number or address. Moses, finished now with his washing, curled up into a tight black ball and shut his eyes. Still wrapped in the duvet, I followed suit and laid wearily on the bed, my head aching from the shock of my otherworldly encounter. The moon had gone from the window and rode high in the sky, shrunken to the size of a pin hole, leaving the bedroom in darkness. So to the sound of the cat's soothing purr, I promptly fell asleep, my last thoughts that I must get in touch with Mum so she could tell her neighbor's aunt where I suspected her cat had gone.

~*~

The offices of Wigglesworth & Horner solicitors were situated on the busy High Street in the center of Whitby, surrounded on both sides by bustling shops. A baker's, The Three Ovens, from which the tantalizing smell of hot pasties wafted on the breeze, was on one side, and a shoe repairer's called Mend Your Sole on the other—what a name! Nervous yet dressed to the nines, if I may say so myself, I arrived for work on my first day.

I wore a smart black trouser suit teamed with a blouse, discreet jewelry, and a slick of red lipstick, not only to match the blouse but to brighten up my somewhat pale washed out face that, however hard I tried, I couldn't do anything about at the moment. My coat, long and black, I shrugged off in the doorway and carried hooked over my arm like the drooping neck of a swan.

A huddle of men deep in conversation was standing in the lobby as I walked in, leaving a fresh and clear but bitingly cold frosty day behind me. If I remembered rightly, the reception was on this floor, the ground floor, through a door to the left of where the men were standing. The practice occupied the whole building, the first and second floors, where all the offices were situated.

One of the men I recognized straight away was Mr. Wigglesworth, the savior who had offered me the job. The other I had never seen before but supposed to be Mr. Horner, a sharp-faced skinny weasel of a man. And the other— Well, the other was quite surprising, absolutely nothing like a man you would expect to see in Whitby on a Monday morning in October. But rather like he should be riding a horse in Texas with a band of cowboys or hobnobbing in the hot desert with Clint Eastwood and a giant cactus.

He was tall and broad chested, extraordinarily handsome, with high cheekbones and piercing green eyes. Yes, I know, it's just like a description of a hero in a romantic story, but it's not an exaggeration—I swear! He wore a black suit with a white shirt and a tie that hung slightly loose so that just a slice of chest was visible to my prying eye. His smart shiny black shoes had long pointed toes, and he carried a briefcase as well as—hmm, now this could be a big mistake—a rather loud grey and yellow checked overcoat draped over one arm.

Now, this was where it got really weird. He wore a Stetson—a Stetson hat! A real cowboy Stetson hat, which he took off and held to his chest, so I was able to see his blond Robert Redford hairstyle in all its glory as

I approached them. At this action, Mr. Wigglesworth turned and, catching sight of me, inclined his head and said, "Ah, Miss Lewis, good morning. How are you? Had a good move, I hope?"

"Yes, very good, thank you." I nodded and held out my hand, which he shook vigorously.

He gave the two other men a brief two finger salute at his temple and then turned to me. "Come, come," he said, indicating with his head.

I followed his narrow figure up a broad sweeping staircase to the first floor, where he showed me straight into his office, the room I recognized straight away, where I'd been interviewed. A ginger and white cat lay huddled in a ball on the window seat, bringing to mind my encounter the previous week with the fluffy black Moses, who now appeared to be my cat, as Mum's neighbor's aunt had denied all knowledge of him. So, where my feline friend had come from, I had no idea. Maybe he was some kind of ghost, a phantom, or merely a part of my otherworldly experience in the mirror.

"Tom, our office cat," Mr. Wigglesworth informed me gravely, making a sweeping gesture with an open hand, and then took a seat behind his desk as I sat down opposite him. His desk was neat and tidy, with just an open laptop and a pile of papers marring the shiny black surface. The room was large and airy, with plenty of light coming through the two arched windows that looked out onto all the comings and goings of the busy High Street.

"Now then, Miss Lewis—"

"Please," I said. "As we're going to be working together, you can call me Chrissie."

"Hmm, yes, that's very kind of you. But—" He gazed up straight into my face. "There's been a change of plan."

"A change of plan?" I asked him, sitting forward in my seat and clutching my bag hard on my lap. I had an awful feeling he was going to say I didn't have a job now. That after my interview, after the terrible mistake they'd made at offering me the job, they'd had second thoughts and decided not to take me on. What else could it be? I'd have to sell the house—go back to Leeming, to the gossip and the snide glances, to watching Stuart canoodling with Anna. I didn't think I could face that, not after everything I'd been through.

"Yes," He gazed at me apologetically. "Due to a change in my personal circumstances, I will be taking a six month's leave of absence from Wigglesworth & Horner almost immediately."

Just for a split second, I thought Mr. Wigglesworth was going to confide in me and tell me the reason for his impending disappearance, but he didn't say anything, and the moment was lost. But nevertheless, my heart rose at those words. Mr. Wigglesworth was leaving, only for a while though, and not me!

"Leaving?" I asked. "Oh, dear. So, what about me?"

"You, my dear Miss Lewis, will have a different boss, a temporary boss, I should say." He gave me such a charming grin, his face looking so young and boyish, that I had serious misgivings about him leaving and being replaced by somebody else.

"Who?" I asked, a frown creasing my forehead.

"His name," he said, rather importantly I thought, "Is Richard Curtis."

The cat suddenly stood up and, arching its back, jumped onto Mr. Wigglesworth's desk, laid itself out long and thin, and began to purr deep down inside its throat as if it were a motor-controlled toy.

"Oh." I couldn't think of anything else to say.

Excitedly he sat forward, his forearms resting on the desk right next to the cat, who didn't move a whisker but carried on with his deep throbbing purr. "He's just arrived from America. Arizona, in fact. He works as a probate lawyer in a firm called Mowlam & Murray in Tucson."

"Oh," I repeated. I didn't like to say, "Oh, you mean the man who wears a Stetson hat?" After all, just because somebody wears a Stetson hat, it doesn't necessarily mean they come from Arizona, does it? Mr. Curtis could well be the other man, the sharp-featured one who I suspected was Mr. Horner.

"I'm sure, dear Miss Lewis—"

"Chrissie," I told him.

"Chrissie." He nodded his head slightly in

acquiescence. "That you and Mr. Curtis will work admirably together. He's an excellent solicitor—well, lawyer, as they say in America—and knows so much about the probate side of things. And I am absolutely sure he will make a very good boss. What do they say? Kind but fair."

I nodded again. I really was beginning to think I was morphing into one of those nodding Churchill dogs that people like to put in the back of their cars.

"Now then, I'll call him in so you can introduce yourselves." He made to rise from his chair but was stopped by a sudden tap at the door. "Come in," said Mr. Wigglesworth with a frown, glancing over his shoulder.

The door swung open, and the man wearing the Stetson hat stood there, a looming dark shape, his broad shoulders filling the doorway. The Stetson was gone, no doubt hanging on a coat stand somewhere, along with his loud checked overcoat. But his hands cradled his hips as if he really was in the Wild West and wearing a holster from which he could spring a gun at any moment.

"Ah, Mr. Curtis, do come in. I was just about to fetch you to meet Miss Lewis, your brand new personal assistant."

"Well, hello there, Miss Lewis," he said in a deep, reverberating drawl. "I'm mighty pleased to meet you." A feeling of total warmth enveloped my body as he grabbed my hand with both of his and shook it hard.

Taking deep breaths to try to stop myself from

shaking—I just hadn't prepared myself for the sheer force and, well, size of him and his personality—I rose unsteadily to my feet and said, "It's good to meet you too, Mr. Curtis."

"Richard," he said with a smile, and I couldn't help but notice the lovely little wrinkles at the corner of his eyes. "Or maybe Rick. I really don't mind."

"Chrissie," I said with a tremor in my voice that surely he must notice. His eyes, grassy green flecked with pieces of flickering gold, stared into mine for what seemed like ages, eons until, with a will of iron, I pulled my gaze away.

"Well then," said Mr. Wigglesworth, clapping his hands together with satisfaction. "That's settled then."

We all nodded around at each other and agreed that yes, it was.

Chapter Two

"You'll have to, Morgan. I don't care what you say—go against my wishes all you like—but you will definitely have to dispose of that cat very soon."

There was a deep throaty chuckle, and then, "Oh brother of mine, do you really think I take notice of your wishes? Moses is my heart and will never leave my side."

"You cause yourself deep trouble then, Morgan. The finger already points at you as a witch, and you flaunt your witch's cat!"

"Seth, listen to yourself. I am no more a witch than—"

"The die is set. You are guilty already."

There was silence then, apart from breathing—deep and heavy, angry breathing, coming from the two people that had somehow got into my cellar and were here now arguing bitterly (well, at least on the young man's side) about witchcraft and cats. The cellar was larger, a lot larger than I'd thought, and in an L shape, so even on reaching the bottom of the steps, I still couldn't see fully into all of it, into all its nooks and crannies. My heart beating hard, I pressed myself against the wall, trying to melt into the shadows, far too wary and afraid to switch on the light. Moving slowly and carefully, I felt my way along the wall like a blind person, the stones rough beneath my palms.

Fumbling in the back pocket of my jeans, I felt for my phone, relieved when my fingers felt the cold hard shape of it. I felt safe knowing it was there, and I could call for help quickly if needed. I regretted not bringing a weapon with me, something I could defend myself with. But, when I was merely taking a look in the cellar of my new home, I didn't think for one minute that it would be necessary.

Keeping my body tight against the wall and deep into the shadows, I could see at last, with a terrible shock, two people, a man and a woman, standing closely together, both clad in dark clothes. Clothes from a long time ago. Medieval perhaps? What was going on? Was it the Whitby Goth weekend, and I hadn't realized?

The woman wore a long black gown with a white apron tied over the top, a fluted bonnet covering her head, beneath which cascaded her long hair, shiny and black as a raven's wing, as they say. She had ruby red lips and flashing green eyes, and her skin was milky white and smooth. She was beautiful and certainly not at all like any witch I'd ever seen before. Definitely nothing like the witch in *The Wizard of Oz,* an ugly old crone with a green face and a large wart on her pointed chin.

"I am innocent until proven guilty," she said carelessly. "You know that, Seth."

I closed my eyes and opened them again, but they were still there, and the cat, too, hugged close to her breasts that rose from the low-cut bodice of her dress. A beautiful black fluffy cat, its orange eyes glowing brightly in the dim. *Why, it's Moses,* I thought. *What on earth are they doing with my cat? They'd better not be trying to steal him.*

I stepped towards them, putting out my arms, intending to take Moses away from this strange woman. He was definitely my cat now, and if they had a problem with that, they could speak to Mum's neighbor's aunt for all I cared. Even though she'd denied all knowledge of him, I was sure she'd back me up and tell them what was what.

"Excuse me, but" My voice came out far too loud in the quiet, but my hands, flailing about now, grasped at nothing but air.

Shocked, I gazed around, my eyes skittering into every dark corner of the cellar—nothing. No medieval looking people, just a small squeaking meow from the floor and the cat looking up at me. I saw the glint of silver from his name tag as I picked him up and hugged him close, reassured now that it really was Moses, but he struggled tetchily and jumped down with a thud, his tail pointing into the air as he sprinted up the stone steps and out of sight.

Taking a deep breath, I stood motionless, too afraid to move, my eyes darting everywhere, looking for the two decidedly strange people who had so definitely been here but had disappeared like smoke wreathing up a chimney. Totally spooked now and craving light and noise, I too turned tail and ran quickly up the steps, shutting the cellar door firmly behind me.

~*~

Thoughts of the evening before and the weird happenings in the cellar occupied my mind as I hurried to work the following morning. I couldn't get the two people I'd seen out of my head—the beautiful girl called Morgan and her brother, Seth. And Moses too. How on earth could a figment of my imagination be holding a real live cat? It was too strange to comprehend. I was fully aware that Whitby was renowned for its spooky past. After all, there was Dracula and the Whitby Witches and the modern-day Goths. But why were these people in my house? Had something happened there in the past? Had they, God help us all, died there?

Hmm, I thought I'd have to do a bit of googling later to see what I could find out, or perhaps I should speak with Mum's neighbor's aunt to see if anything ghostly had happened in the house while she was living there. The more I thought about it, though, the more outlandish it seemed. I mean, after all, how was it possible that two medieval people could be talking to each other in my cellar? I had suspected they were from the Whitby Goth weekend, but that was the next week. So, put all that with the weird black figure I thought I'd seen in the mirror, and none of it made any sense at all. Really, it was probably better that I mull it over later that night when the second day at my new job was well and truly in the past.

Whitby town center was already busy on that bright, frosty morning. People formed a long straggly queue into the Three Ovens bakers to buy their breakfast hot sandwiches and coffees, the odor of which hung in the air mixed tantalizingly with the smell of frying bacon and flaky croissants. A stiff breeze blew in from the sea, and seagulls cawed overhead as people, looking like little black dots in the distance, walked on the sands, shoulders hunched against the cold, dogs bounding along beside them.

That beach will be crowded in the summer, I thought idly to myself. And how different Whitby would be then, with sightseers and holiday makers all crowding in to visit the abbey and the 199 steps, to look around the quirky souvenir shops and to sample Whitby's delicious fish and chips. I'd better make the most of it now, while it was a bit quieter and there was room to move around and do some more sightseeing of my own. I still had such a lot to do.

My thoughts turned back to yesterday and the kindness of Mr. Wigglesworth as he introduced me to everybody in the offices of Wigglesworth & Horner. And of course, my temporary boss, Richard Curtis, (Hey Miss Chrissie, you can call me Rick, you know, I really don't mind) who fascinated and astounded me all at the same time. All I could say at the present time was that I thought working with him would be very...um, what was the word? Interesting, to say the least. Especially as we were working on the death and destruction side of the business—probate.

I loved the bright, airy office I shared with the two other PAs. Milly Robbins worked for Mr. Horner, the sharp-faced weasel of a man who was talking to Richard Curtis and Mr. Wigglesworth when I arrived at the offices only yesterday. It seemed years ago now. Yes, Mr. Horner—now he was a turn up for the books. A brash Londoner, full of jokes and funny stories. Oh yes, quite the comedian was our Pete Horner, totally belying his looks. His expertise was in the conveyancing side of the practice.

Milly, I thought, was a little older than me, maybe early thirties. She had shoulder length auburn hair and wore bright red lipstick. While watching her type, the fastest I'd ever seen in my life, I saw the flash of a ring on the third finger of her left hand. I felt a sudden pang of envy at the fact she was married, maybe to the love of her life. Unlike me, who'd been dumped unceremoniously before even setting foot in a church. It was very unlikely at the moment that I'd ever make it to the altar.

Then there was Norman Ross, PA for the matrimonial solicitor, Lily Makepeace, who wore her thin iron-grey hair elaborately coiffed into a little cottage loaf bun and wore flat brogue shoes and tweed suits. Her overall look made me feel like a catwalk glamour puss—which could only be a good thing, right? I'd never in my life known anybody who made me feel that way.

Norman was young and skinny—"turn sideways and he disappears," as my old grandad used to say—but very willing and capable, chatty too. But unfortunately for him, he had such a bad case of acne that his face resembled the pock ridden surface of the moon. *The moon*, I thought with a shudder that *sometimes peers like a cold face through my bedroom window, scaring me half to death.* But that's another story. He also had a blindingly red nose and a perpetual sniff which, from the look on Milly's face at times, drove her around the bend.

Pat Gianni was the receptionist, the face of Wigglesworth & Horner. She had an Italian husband, so she always shouted "mamma mia" and threw her hands in the air when a problem arose. She tended to wear tight fitting soft woolly jumpers in shades of baby blue and pink teamed with smart midi length skirts and always a thin gold or silver belt cinching her waist. Oh yes, and she ate margarita pizza with extra cheese every day for lunch.

And last but by no means least was our gofer, Layla Moss—a good name for a weed killer, perhaps?—a Whitby

Goth by the look of her, black lipstick being slightly off putting during the day. But very efficient, excellent at the photocopying and filing, and even better if you fancied a pasty or sandwich from the baker's next door but couldn't be bothered to get up off your—

So there it is, the whole cast of Wigglesworth & Horner. People that at the moment appeared to be so friendly and kind. What my real role there would become, I had no idea, especially with a boss like Mr. Richard "Texan" Curtis. But I was sure it was going to be fun finding out, and as long as he didn't gaze at me again with those mesmerizing glassy green eyes, then everything should be hunky dory. Not forgetting, of course, that I had zero interest in men at the moment and that whatever the circumstances, Mr. Richard Curtis would get nowhere with me. So, the stage was set, and the curtain rising albeit at a slightly lopsided angle. So let the show begin.

~*~

His office door was wide open, propped open, I noticed, with a cast iron figurine of a black cat, paws raised and green eyes glowing, a mischievous grin on its face. What was it with Whitby and black cats? And where had this one come from? Sunny Arizona? Or one of the many little gift shops on the High Street right here in Whitby? Peering in, I could see him, Richard Curtis, sitting at his desk—well, Mr. Wigglesworth's desk really—gazing with fascination at the screen of a laptop. The office was tidy and, apart from the obvious desk and chair—and a spare one for me, I suppose, plus a tall chrome lamp in a corner—only a filing cabinet stood against one wall, a pile of buff and blue colored files laid on top of it. Oh, there was an old wooden coat stand too, where the Stetson hat and the loud checked overcoat hung in all their glory. Behind him, the large arched windows showed a bright blue sky streaked with smoky tendrils of cloud.

The thought, *I wonder why he's here*? came to mind. Had something happened in Arizona for him to want to leave his life, his family, whatever he had going on for six months? I gave a tentative knock and Richard Curtis, looking up straightaway, said, "Well, hello there, Miss Chrissie." And then, standing up and moving towards me stealthily and sleek as a panther, he said, "Come in, come in. We don't stand on ceremony here." He reached out and once again enveloped my small hand within his two large warm ones. "It sure is good to see you again, Miss Chrissie. Please sit down."

He indicated a chair opposite him, on the other side of the desk from where he now resumed his seat, where I sat willingly, my knees, for some strange reason, feeling quite weak and wobbly and bendy as Plasticine. I gazed at him, taking in the stubbly light beard that grew on his cheeks and his chin, as well as his mesmerizing green eyes and silky blond hair. All the things I'd almost forgotten from yesterday's meeting. Or had I?

"I just want to say, Miss Chrissie, that I didn't know until yesterday that you had no idea about Mr. Wigglesworth leaving the practice."

"No, I didn't," I told him. "When I came for the interview, as far as I was aware, Mr. Wigglesworth was going to be my boss."

"Yeah, well, I hope I can live up to your expectations of what a good boss ought to be, Miss Chrissie."

"Oh, I'm sure you'll be great, Rick. But please, you don't need to call me Miss Chrissie. Just Chrissie is fine."

"*Just* Chrissie? And not *Miss* Chrissie?"

I had to smile. "Chrissie. Nothing else, Chrissie."

"Okay, ma'am." He gave a blindingly white smile and, leaning forward, forearms on the desk, said, "I suppose where I come from in Arizona, most ladies are called Miss in front of their names. You have different rules here."

"Yes," I agreed. "I suppose we do. Unless we work in a school, where the children call the ladies Miss. But I've never been to Arizona. In fact, apart from a trip to New York a few years ago, I've not been anywhere in America."

"Oh wow. New York is great but crazy! Not anywhere else in America? Wow. Well, I'll tell you a little secret, shall I? Until now, I'd never been anywhere in England. This is my first time, so to speak." He gave another mega-watt smile, making my heart rate increase at an astounding rate.

"Do you like it?" I asked him.

"Oh yeah, it's a pretty country. Friendly too." He gave another smile. "Small though," he added. He pushed a lock of blond hair back from his forehead, once again causing my heart to rev up a beat. "Do you come from here in Whitby, Chrissie?"

"No, I was born in a little village called Leeming in West Yorkshire. A couple of hours drive away from here."

He frowned and said, "Is that near London?"

"No." I smiled and shook my head. "London is in the south of England, Leeming is in the North. Have you heard of Haworth?"

"Haworth? Yeah, I love those books, *Jane Eyre* and *Wuthering Heights*. Um, those girls, what are they called? Their name escapes me." He put his fingertips to his temple and shook his head.

"The Bronte sisters?"

"Yeah, really cool. I love all that stuff. The history here in England is astounding, and oh my God, your queen! She's one hell of a gal."

I smiled and said, "Yes, she certainly is. You mentioned London before. Well, the queen lives there, but Leeming, where I was born, is near Haworth."

Manic typing suddenly sounded from the main office—it had to be Milly, the fastest typist in the north—reminding me of why I'd come in to see Richard Curtis in the first place, which was to see if he had any work for me to do. Interested in carrying on the conversation but conscious that I was taking up too much of his time, I said, "I came in here to see if you had any work for me to do."

"Yeah, sure I have. I've been doing some dictation. There's a couple of clients wanting wills drafted out." He fixed me with his beautiful glassy green eyes as he stood up. "There's some really wild bequests, you know, Chrissie. Should make for some interesting work for you." He indicated with a nod of his blond head. "The folders you'll need are over there on top of the filing cabinet."

I rose to my feet and collected the files, clutching them to my chest like a shield as I made to go out of the room. But catching sight once again of the cast iron cat, I asked him, "Is this yours? I didn't notice it yesterday when Mr. Wigglesworth was here."

"Yeah, I bought it just the other day in a cute little gift shop on the High Street just along here." He indicated randomly towards the window with an outstretched hand whilst walking around his desk again and strolling over to me, his footsteps leaving soft imprints on the carpet and the scent of the musky cologne he wore becoming stronger as he came nearer.

"I assume you like cats, then?"

"Oh yeah, I do—got three back home, Theo, Milo, and Jasper, great boys, all of them. Do you?"

I told him the tale of Moses, the black cat suddenly appearing from nowhere at the house I'd just moved into and scaring me half to death. I didn't tell him about the two medieval people I thought I'd seen in my cellar, though. I certainly didn't want him to think his new personal assistant was some sort of raving lunatic.

He laughed out loud at the story. "Ha, a Whitby Witch cat, eh?"

"You said your cats were back home? Do you mean in Arizona or here in Whitby? Obviously, you have a place here too."

Oh my God, what was I saying? I felt my cheeks burning hot and red. I didn't want him to think I was trying to find out where he lived.

But he didn't seem to notice and just said, "In Arizona. My brother, Chase, is taking care of them for me. He's got a wife and two kids, two dogs, and two cats of his own, but he still offered to take my boys in. He's a great guy."

He gave me a smile so charming I felt as if I was floating as I returned to the office, where I sat down in a daze, placing the buff files on my desk. The radiator next to me hummed softly, filling the room with warmth, and outside the window, gulls wheeled in the sky like little white phantoms.

"Good meeting with the cowboy?" asked Milly with a knowing smile.

"You mean Mr. Curtis?" I replied nonchalantly. "Very good, thank you. I've plenty of work to do, at least." I busied myself with the files, hoping my racing heart would calm just a little bit.

"Yeah, I bet you have," she said with a friendly grin, which to my way of thinking, didn't quite go with the comment. A stab at a bit of innuendo, I suspected, but in the course of time, I would certainly let her know, as well as everybody else, that men were totally off limits to me at the moment, especially Mr. Richard Curtis.

Norman Ross, a cheeky grin almost splitting his ravaged face in two, stood up and shouted, "Ride 'em, cowboy, whoa, whoa!" whilst swinging an imaginary lasso in circles with an outstretched arm.

"Totally inappropriate, Norman," said Milly, giving him the dead eye.

"Yeah, I totally agree, Milly," was Layla's response as she staggered through the door, just in time to hear Norman's comment, a great pile of photocopying in her arms. "We must apologize, Chrissie, on Norman's behalf."

"What's all this?" whined Norman, crossing his skinny arms across his equally skinny chest. "Naughty Norman always in the wrong, eh?" He gave a great loud offended sniff.

"You should think before you open your big mouth," Layla shot back at him as she proceeded to stalk around the room distributing the photocopying, some of which she laid carefully on my desk, as well as on Norman's and Milly's. In her long black skirt, she reminded me, with a stab of uneasiness, of the medieval people I thought I'd seen in my cellar.

"Oh please," I said to them all. "I'm not insulted at all. I know that Norman was only joking."

"Oh really," he said slyly. "Is that what you think?"

"Yes," I said, directing my gaze solely at Norman. "I think you were having a bit of a laugh, Norman, which is fine. I like office banter. But," and looking at all three now, I said, "As I will be purely *working* for Mr. Curtis, nothing else, no double-edged comments, please. Thank you." There! That should put them all in their place.

Both Milly and Layla nodded their heads as if to say, "Yeah, okay, we get it," while Norman, a cowed expression on his face, plugged in his earphones and began to type really fast, almost as fast as Milly, although only two of his fingers stabbed rapidly at the keyboard. I knew then without a doubt that, however long it lasted, my working life at Wigglesworth & Horner was going to be quite all right—as long as I kept away from the cowboy! And watched out for Norman. I didn't know what it was, but there was just something about Norman.

~*~

Here we go, I thought, *let's see what I can find out.* I brought my laptop to life and, on finding google, quickly typed in the words *The Whitby Witches.* Three names popped up on the screen—Old Kattie, Anne Pierson, and Mad Maggie, but definitely no Morgan. I briefly read about each of the witches, thinking, *Oh my God, were there really people like that in Whitby?* It also brought up a trilogy of books called, unusually, *The Whitby Witches*. The books looked really good, and I made a mental note to have a read of them at some point. I carried on googling, trying to find out something about Morgan and her brother, Seth, and why I'd imagined them in my cellar. There must be a reason, but what? I tried all different combinations of words—Witch Morgan, Morgan Witch, Black cats, Whitby Morgan, Morgan Whitby.

Stumped, I sat there for a minute or two, simply staring at the screen of my laptop, disappointed and unsure what to do next. Maybe I should give up. After all, I must have imagined it. There was no way those two people could have been real. No way at all.

Moses jumped up and tried to squeeze his way onto my lap, purring loudly. I picked him up and hugged him close, reveling in the softness of his fur and his smell, clean and fresh, as if he'd been washed and sprayed with *Febreeze*. I put him on my lap, where he promptly curled into a ball and closed his eyes. Putting the laptop next to me on the settee to make room for the cat, I found the google bar again and idly typed in Pear Tree Cottage. If I couldn't find out anything about Morgan and her brother, Seth, I could at least acquaint myself with the history of the house I was living in.

Interesting information appeared on the screen indicating that the house was a grade two listed building, and there were a few pictures of the outside of the property showing a rutted track in front instead of the road that was there now. I noticed that the house and even the garden looked almost the same, with its small square of scrubby grass surrounded by bushes and what looked to be clumps of daffodils in the borders. Looking closely at the picture, the pear tree was now clearly visible, its branches bowed almost to the ground by the weight of the fruit hanging from them. I felt a pang of nostalgia for the tree and its yearly harvest of pears, no doubt used at that time for making pies and cakes and crumbles and sweet tasting heady wine.

Scrolling down the screen, there was a further article which gave a potted history of the previous occupants, listing them in name and the years in which they had lived there. I noticed an Earnshaw, a Carter, a Williams, and a Spink, but one of the first families to live there was called Bloom—Ingrid and Asa Bloom. And this was definitely where my heart rate started revving up—almost as much as it had when Richard Curtis looked at me long and hard with his sea-green eyes—when I saw these words. "Along with their two children, Morgan and Seth Bloom."

It couldn't be true. I must have been imagining things again. But no, I read the same line over and over again just to make sure. "Along with their two children, Morgan and Seth Bloom." Morgan and Seth, my two ghostly visitors to the cellar. A coincidence? Two names as unusual as that?

My hands shaking. I scrolled further down.

Morgan Bloom, known as the only true Whitby beauty, was also a witch. Proven beyond doubt. Stunning, with long black hair and flashing green eyes, she had flawless white skin and an enigmatic smile, which she used to entice the males of the village into her arms. Many poor unfortunates fell under her spell, causing much jealousy from wives and sweethearts alike. Her brother, Seth, also had an unusual beauty for a man that attracted ladies like moths to a light, marred only by a large black mole that grew on the soft skin beneath his left eye. There were suspicions that he was a changeling or a werewolf because of his strange yellow eyes flecked with black, like pieces of charcoal on onyx.

Morgan Bloom was suspected of witchcraft as she carried her familiar Moses, a black cat, with her at all times tucked into the bodice of her dress or carried in a cloth bag worn tight around her body. She made strange brews suspected as love potions and spells and gave it to many persons, mainly males, to drink – she said to ward off the evils of ill health. She was seen studying the lines on the palms of hands, including those of her brother, Seth Bloom, and her mother and father, Ingrid and Asa Bloom. It was suspected she told fortunes and happenings of the future and conjured demons out of thin air.

After months of frantic hiding for her life, aided by her brother Seth, she was cruelly tracked down and murdered by an unruly mob of villagers on a perishing dark night in October c1700. After being tried as a witch, the mob waited and watched on the cold sandy shore until she could float no more in the restless Whitby Sea. The other three members of the family perished too by fire, only a handful of months later, trapped in their home, Pear Tree Cottage, and the house and garden were annihilated and burnt. Note, please, by all that is true that the bodies of the family were never found.

Part of the house, Pear Tree Cottage, was rebuilt, and the garden, although it withered and perished, grew back eventually, except for its beautiful namesake, the pear tree. Even though a stump of the great tree, blackened and burnt, still stood after the fire, it never again reached its previous glory but died slowly into the earth, never to flourish again, as did the flesh and the bones of the Bloom family. God rest their souls and those of the almighty angels.

Mystified, I simply stared at the screen of my laptop, conscious of Moses, Morgan's familiar, curled in a tight pulsing ball on my lap. I was very conscious of my surroundings—the sitting room growing dark now as the light faded outside, emphasizing its creepy dark corners and the fire that crackled bright orange and red in the hearth, its tongues of flame disappearing mysteriously up the chimney; the ancient black beams that crisscrossed the ceiling; and the oval mirror that hung above the fireplace, where I'd caught a glimpse of the scary black shape only a few days before.

Vampires and fluttering bats and a black cloaked Dracula raced through my mind until, with a sudden movement that startled the cat, I jumped up and ran around the room, switching on all the lamps and pulling the curtains to shut out the blackness that loomed at the window. There was only one thing to do—I needed to speak to Mum. She'd contacted her neighbor's aunt before when I'd asked her to enquire about Moses, but this time I wanted to speak to her directly. Surely she would have knowledge of the history of Pear Tree Cottage. Picking up my mobile, I pressed the buttons to make the call.

Chapter Three

I almost tripped over a dish on my doorstep as I left the house to go to work the next day, still jittery from last night and the information I'd read about Morgan and Seth Bloom and the history of Pear Tree Cottage. It had made for a long restless night. Bending down, I picked it up, and as I peeled back the foil keeping it warm, the unmistakable smell of pears drifted towards me. I inhaled it dreamily, almost tasting the sweet nuttiness of the fruit. And then, with a start, I wondered where on earth it had come from.

A movement caught my eye, and I saw something, a tiny figure, scurrying up next door's garden path. Was this the neighbor who stared at me through the window on the day I moved in? Now the bearer of gifts?

"Hello," I shouted out. "Excuse me!" Clutching the dish, I ran over to the fence that divided our gardens and peered over, but the leafy branches of a spreading lilac bush obscured my view. So I stood on my tiptoes looking for her, craning my neck and turning my head from side to side.

"Excuse me?" I said again, and the figure stopped its scurrying and stood still at the front door, one hand on the doorknob as if to go inside. I could see her now, though, a tiny, skinny lady, bird like in appearance, with darting black eyes in her little face. So much like a robin, resplendent in her fluffy red jumper and smart black trousers.

"Thank you," I said, holding up the dish, "For the pie. It smells delicious."

"That's quite all right, dear," she said, turning to face me. "A welcome to your new home gift." She moved nearer the fence and put her tiny claw like hand through the leafy branches, "Mabel Montgomery, dear, pleased to meet you."

"Pleased to meet you too," I said, shaking her hand whilst juggling awkwardly with the dish. "I'm Chrissie Lewis. The pie is obviously pear—such a lovely smell. Do you have a pear tree?" I asked with a giggle. "Or are they shop bought?"

Looking quite scandalized, she said, "Oh no, dear, I would never use shop bought pears, not when I've got such a lovely big tree in my backyard and so much fruit for the taking. Even though, really, you're the one that's supposed to have it. From what I heard, it never would grow again in your garden after the fire and everything."

"You have a pear tree in your backyard?" I asked

her.

She nodded. "Yes, it grew right up through the flags years ago. Come on in, and I'll show you."

Checking my watch, I said, "I have to go to work now, or I'll be late. Another time?"

"Any time, dear. Only day I'm not in is Tuesday. I always visit my sister in Scarborough on Tuesday. Apart from that—" She gave a casual wave of her hand as she opened the door and made to go inside.

"I'm going to take the pie to work," I shouted after her. "My new colleagues will appreciate it, I'm sure."

"Oh," she said, turning back, "Talking of colleague's, dear, I know one of yours—Lily Makepeace. She's just joined our over sixty club." She gave a cheery wave and disappeared inside the gaping black hole of her doorway.

Now how does she know where I work? I thought as I hurried down the street, slipping and sliding a little on the frosty path that shimmered like silver in the weak sunlight, my mind reeling even more now at what Mabel Montgomery had told me about the pear tree. How weird that it was growing in her garden and not mine. And she also mentioned the fire, so she must know about Pear Tree Cottage's history too. Clutching the still warm dish, the smell of pears following me, I made my way onto the High Street, the usual clamor of cawing seagulls swooping and diving overhead. *Well, if they think they're going to get a taste of my pie, they're much mistaken.*

Another worry flitted through my mind as I approached Wigglesworth & Horner. I hadn't been able to get in touch with Mum last night, which was bothering me a little as she usually answered her phone straight away. I really needed to speak to her neighbor's aunt too. Oh well, just another thing to add to my list of "something's not quite right, but what?" list.

As I entered the building, Pat shouted out a cheerful "Buon giorno," which I took to mean good morning in Italian. I stopped briefly and carefully peeled back the foil to show her the pie, at which she gesticulated wildly with her fingers to her lips, saying the words "bon appetite" over and over again. I said she was welcome to her share at coffee time before taking the stairs at a gallop.

I needn't have hurried because the office was empty, with no sign of Milly pecking at her keyboard in a manic spate of typing or Layla stalking about with piles of papers drooping from her arms, her lips glossy black and pouting. Even Norman's chair was empty, although at an odd angle, and the papers on his desk were in disarray as if a hurricane had swept through overnight.

Dumping my bag on my desk and taking the still warm, sweet-smelling pie, I made my way through to the kitchen, noticing as I went past that the door to the little room called the "safe room" was open. This was where the massive cast iron safe was kept, along with packets of house deeds and wills stored on shelves in strict alphabetical order. There was also an old biscuit tin that was never locked away in the big safe—everybody is trustworthy, right?—containing petty cash and savings for very important things like Christmas do's and staff nights out. The room was usually kept locked, but now it was open and must have been like that all night, as it seemed I was the first one in the office.

There was a muffled cough, a sniff, which sounded very familiar to my ears, as I was sure it would to Milly's too if she were here. Creeping from the kitchen, I peered around the "safe room" door, narrowing my eyes while they became accustomed to the dark shadows inside. Gradually the inside of the little room became clearer, and I could see the old wrinkled brown packages pushed tight together on the shelving and the great big safe with its intricate locking mechanism and huge silver handle on the door. There was an old, mildewy, musty smell.

I could just about make out a figure, its back to me, narrow shoulders hunched, and then I heard that sniffing again, along with the chink of coins and the rustle of papers as, to my shocked eyes, whoever it was—and maybe I could hazard a good guess—stuffed the notes and the coins into the voluminous pockets of their overcoat. What on earth was going on?

Frowning and peering further in, I said, "Norman?"

The figure visibly jumped and sprang around to face me. He looked startled, his eyes wide in his pock marked face.

"What are you doing?" I asked him.

"Nothing," he said defensively, and then obviously thinking better of his reply, said, "Putting money in the tin."

"Why don't you put the light on?" I asked as I pulled the cord, so the overhead strip light sputtered to life, lighting up the room. Now I could clearly see, on the shelf that jutted over the safe, the open petty cash tin, its lid beside it, and a mess of coins and bank notes scattered all over the surface. Glancing at his bulging pockets, I said, "Norman, don't you think you'd better put that money back in the tin?"

"What money?" he said nastily and then patted his pockets. "This? This is my money." He turned around and began to scoop the coins and notes that were still on the shelf into his hand, returning them to the tin and pressing the lid back on with a click.

"I saw—"

He butted in angrily, standing right there in front of me, his hands on his hips, and his cheeks and nose red from the acne and the perpetual cold. "What, Chrissie? What did you see? Prove it," and barged past, knocking me out of the way in his haste to get away and back to the office.

I held back, not sure if Milly and Layla had turned up and would be in the office now and what I would say if they were. They'd probably be able to tell just from looking at my face that something was wrong. I hadn't been able to see that well into the darkened room, but I was pretty sure he'd put some money from the tin into his own pockets. He was right though, I would have difficulty proving it.

Maybe I should tell Richard "Texan" Curtis. After all, that's what bosses were for. But something held me back. I didn't want to be a snitch in my new job. I didn't know what to do. Norman had me at a disadvantage here, and the awful thought, h*as he done this before*? flitted through my mind. Whatever, I'd been right about one thing—there certainly was something about Norman. And it wasn't good.

~*~

I arrived home that evening half downhearted and half pretty well happy and content—yeah, between a high and a low. Maybe this was what it was like to be Dr. Jekyll and Mr. Hyde? I was downhearted because of the episode with Norman and not knowing what to do about it. But on a high because of my new boss—the man from Arizona himself, Mr. Richard Curtis. I knew I shouldn't be—after all, I had sworn off men at the moment. But he was so kind and understanding when I spoke to him today about all the worries and woes that had accumulated since I'd moved into Pear Tree Cottage.

I hadn't confided in him about Norman. I made no mention of that, although I very nearly did when I first went into the office on the pretense that I was "catching up with the filing," I was that strung up about it. And then I had to deal with an angry Layla, which did nothing to improve my mood.

"Hey, that's my job," she said angrily, standing in front of me, hands on hips—just as Norman had earlier—when she saw me taking a pile of papers out of the tray clearly marked, "Filing for Mr. Wigglesworth." (She hadn't had time to change the sign as yet). But I told her I needed the papers for an important meeting, and so, finally, she let me off with a stern reprimand that, "No way in the future are you allowed to touch the filing, Chrissie."

He was sitting at his desk, busily talking on the phone to a new client, advising him on certain bequests he wanted to add to his will. "Yeah, Mr. Rogers. But which amount to your wife?" And then, after a short silence, "Oh right, the larger sum to your dog? Penelope?" Followed by a raising of the eyebrows and a wink in my direction. My head couldn't quite cope with that one, I can tell you. But then again, I was pretty sure that if I'd stayed with Stuart, he would have thought nothing of leaving all his worldly goods to the animals on his mum and dad's farm rather than to me.

"Well, that was a funny one," he said with a laugh after he'd finished his phone call with Mr. Rogers. "He's leaving more in his will to his dog than his wife. Strange!"

"Dogs can be very loyal, affectionate companions,"

I told him as I opened the filing cabinet and proceeded to search amongst the letter "N." I had some papers for the Norris file.

"Hmm, yeah, and maybe the wife isn't so loyal and affectionate, eh?" He grinned at this comment, but it set me thinking again as to why he was here. What had made him travel so far away from Arizona? After all, he couldn't have gone much further—well, apart from Australia, I suppose. Was he running away from something? A woman, perhaps? He hadn't mentioned a woman when he'd told me about his cats being left with his brother.

We both carried on working quietly and steadily, the only sounds in the room the ticking of a large grandmother clock that Rick must have brought with him that now stood in a corner near his desk. The clock was a pretty thing, with long golden hands that moved relentlessly around its heart shaped face and had beautiful flowers carved artfully all along the length of its shiny wooden body. There was the faint hum of traffic from the High Street, and of course, the usual cawing and screeching of the gulls as they swooped past the window, occasionally tapping on the glass with their beaks and making us jump. I was sure they did it on purpose. Tom, the office cat, was still snoozing, curled up on the window seat.

Noises from the office were muted from here—Milly's typing and the ringing of the phones, Norman's occasional bray of laughter (although what he had to laugh about I had no idea) and the twittering of Lily Makepeace, similar in her bird like ways to my neighbor and her fellow over sixty club member, Mabel Montgomery, although more like a little brown wren than a red breasted robin. I caught a loud guffaw from Pete Horner, followed by a tirade of London slang like somebody shouting on a market stall in Shepherd's Bush that made me shake my head in bewilderment. "Apples and pears," "Cup a rosie lee," "Give us a monkey, give us a pony." What a strange one he was. Obviously thought he was some sort of comedian.

Rick's deep voice finally interrupted my thoughts, "Hey, you okay there today, Chrissie? You're very quiet."

Busily looking through the "Bs" now, I turned to face him and said, "Yes, I'm fine, I...." But his expression was so caring and his voice so soothing that I said, "Well, actually, I've a few worries since moving into my new place. So don't mind me if I'm quiet sometimes."

"Hey, come and sit over here." He nodded his blond head towards the chair in front of his desk. "Maybe it will help to talk." He got up and perched himself on the edge of his desk where his thighs, encased tightly within his smart suit trousers, were very close to me. The scent of his musky aftershave hovered all around, making my temperature rise and my heartbeat increase at a rapid rate.

"Now, what's the problem then, Chrissie?"

"Well, I don't like to take up your time. I—"

"Hey, no worries. I'm your boss. If you've problems

at work, then you can unburden to your boss." He waved his hands expansively.

For just a split second, I had an overwhelming desire to tell him about Norman and what I was almost sure I'd seen that morning in the "safe room." But instead said, "It's not about work though, Richard…um, Rick. It's my house. I think it's haunted."

"Hey, Chrissie, unload."

And I went on to tell him everything, all about the information I'd found online about Morgan and Seth Bloom, about witchcraft and drownings and black cats and pear trees, as well as the strange hooded figure I'd seen in the mirror. The words came tumbling from my mouth one after another, just like the juicy fruit that fell from the branches of the pear tree and littered the stone flags in Mabel's backyard.

I noticed that his sexy green eyes opened wider and wider as I carried on with my tale, and when I told him I thought I'd seen Morgan and Seth Bloom in my cellar, Morgan cradling a real live Moses the cat, he shook his head in disbelief.

"I know it's hard to believe," I said. "But—"

"No, I don't find it hard to believe, Chrissie, God knows there's strange goings on everywhere, and your house is old, real old." He shifted a bit on the desk and pulled his trousers up slightly at the knee, and then leaned forward, closer to me, putting his forearm on his thigh. I couldn't help but gaze into his green eyes that I noticed now were flecked with tiny specks of gold. "I've plenty of stories about Arizona. In fact, I'll tell you some spooky tales right now." He gave an impish grin and began talking. "There's the Birdcage Theatre in a place called Tombstone in Arizona—"

"Tombstone?" I said in wonder. "Is there really such a place as Tombstone? What an eerie name."

"Yeah, there sure is, oh yes siree. It was founded in 1879. What's interesting is that one of the Boothill Cemeteries, so called because most of those buried there had 'died with their boots on,' so to speak, is in Tombstone. Three men killed in the OK Corral shootout are interred there." He gave a short bark of laughter at the, no doubt, horrified expression on my face.

"Anyway, back to the Birdcage Theatre. Back in the day, it would have been the prime entertainment spot in Tombstone, but now it's just an old abandoned building in which there's been ghostly sightings, disembodied voices, and ethereal music." He rolled his eyes, and I gave a great shudder, hunching my shoulders to my ears.

"And then," he said in a low, scary voice, "There's the Copper Queen Hotel. Now prepare yourself for this, Chrissie." He raised his eyebrows, and we grinned at each other. "There's believed to be not one, but three ghosts in the Copper Queen Hotel. The first is an older gentleman who has long hair and a beard and is accompanied by the smell of cigar smoke. He makes an appearance on the fourth floor only, usually as just a shadow."

"If he's just a shadow," I whispered, "How do they know he's an old gentleman?" I'd noticed that his lips were really very red and juicy looking, like a ripe strawberry, and that his teeth were very white and even.

"Hmm, I'm not sure about that," he whispered back. "Um, we'll come to that. Let's move on." He gave another impish grin and then said suddenly, "There's a little ghost boy as well. People say they've heard giggling and the pattering of childish footsteps. Apparently, he drowned in the San Pedro River but is attached to the hotel because his parents used to work there."

"Oh my God! How weird. Poor little boy. Who's the third ghost?"

"Ah, well, the third and probably the most famous is the spirit of a one-time prostitute named Julia Lowell."

"A prostitute?" I said. We were so close to each other now, our faces almost touching, that if we really wanted to, we could have kissed. His luscious strawberry lips were very close to mine.

"Uh huh. It's believed that she used the hotel to visit with her clients, but she ended up falling in love with one of the men."

"Oh no!"

"Uh huh. And when he told her he no longer wanted to see her, she took her own life in the bathtub in her hotel room."

"Oh no. How sad! Poor Julia."

The office had become very dark while we'd been talking, and rain pattered on the window. The sky looked dull and threatening, hung with heavy black clouds. My heart was beating very fast, and my limbs felt limp and heavy. I really couldn't imagine actually standing up and leaving the room.

Suddenly the phone rang, shattering the silence. It trilled and trilled like a bird in the dawn chorus. Rick reached for the receiver, but it was too late, for the ringing stopped.

"Yeah. I, Chrissie—"

Whatever he was going to say was lost forever because Pat's irritated face suddenly poked around the door, and she said sternly, "Your eleven o'clock appointment is here, Mr. Curtis. I've put them in reception. Mr. and Mrs. Ross."

We both jumped up straightaway, Rick fumbling for the light switch and humbly thanking Pat at the same time, while I ran to the filing cabinet and began to search for the Ross file, which I quickly put on his desk and asked if he would like coffee for himself and his clients. I also told him about the pie I'd brought in and that I'd bring some with the coffee.

"Hey, that'll be great. Thank you, Chrissie."

"Thank you for the stories," I said quietly. "You've cheered me up."

"Gee, I hope so," he replied, ducking his head in what seemed like embarrassment. I nodded and made to go out of the room when he said, "Oh, Chrissie, I'll fetch Mr.and Mrs. Ross from reception while you're getting the coffee."

These were the thoughts keeping me company that evening as I climbed the steep hill from Whitby town center, walked along the garden path, and let myself into Pear Tree Cottage. Except for the episode with Norman and maybe the bit with Layla, I was filled with a warmth and happiness I hadn't felt for a long time—not since the early days with Stuart, really. Indoors all was quiet and still except for the frantic meowing of Moses, no doubt telling me he was hungry. I picked him up and hugged him close, but he struggled in my arms and, jumping down with a thud, ran into the kitchen as if to say, "I'm hungry, hooman, feed me!"

Shrugging off my coat, I hung it on one of the little ornate pegs in the hallway and, after feeding Moses, who ate as if he'd been starving for a year, I went into the sitting room. Once ensconced comfortably on my big squashy sofa, I rang Mum again, but still no reply. I let it ring and ring and ring. Where was she? I had no other way of getting in touch. She'd gotten rid of her home phone ages ago because she didn't use it anymore, and she'd never had a computer, so, obviously, had no email address.

Restlessly I moved around the room, touching my

favorite ornaments and putting them back in place, idly glancing at the pictures that hung on the walls, all the time avoiding looking in the mirror—definitely going nowhere near the mirror. Maybe I should take it down and hide it away somewhere. I pulled the curtains against the blackness outside and, feeling chilly, tried to light the fire, but it wouldn't catch and smoldered fitfully in the hearth, sending little red sparks and dense black smoke puffing up the chimney. Moses, sated now and sleepy, joined me on the settee. He sat down and began to wash himself thoroughly with his little pink tongue.

I sank down then, my head in my hands, my happy mood of earlier totally gone away. A sudden terrible feeling of loneliness overcame me, and a hot wave of panic seemed to shoot through my body, just like the fire that had engulfed this very house so many years before. I had nobody, nobody at all. Mum wasn't answering her phone, and my boyfriend of more than six years had dumped me for another woman. I'd had friends in Leeming but had lost contact since I'd moved to Whitby. Which, okay, I regretted now, but all I wanted at the time was to get away from there and have a fresh start. But now I was alone, totally alone.

I felt reassured somehow, though, by the thought of my new boss and his kindness today. For, after all, wouldn't he be feeling lonely too? He was such a long way from any family or friends he might have left behind in

Arizona. Thinking of him gave me the urge to gaze into his green eyes or press my palm against the stubble on his chin, or even run my fingers through the silky blondness of his hair whilst listening to his deep Texan drawl as he told me spooky stories. Ah. Was it my loneliness making me feel that way?

I felt a dipping of my heart at the thought of Norman and what I'd seen him do today, but a faint reassurance because of Milly or perhaps Layla, who I felt I could be friends with in time. But for now, that incredible loneliness was coursing through my body and almost bringing me to tears.

Sniffing, I reached for Moses, who, sleepy and soft, didn't object when I picked him up and, sitting cross-legged on the hearth rug hoping that the fire would catch, cuddled him close. Suddenly, with no warning, a chill swept quickly through the room, making me shiver, and a gauzy white mist appeared in front of me. It rose and hovered above my head, swaying and sweeping and undulating, until long smoky fingers reached down and plucked the sleeping cat from my grasp. It said, in a thin ethereal voice like wind chimes in a breeze, "Moses is my familiar…not yours!" To my astonished eyes, the mist took the trembling shape of a woman, a terrible smile on her face making her appear sinister and ugly. I was able to see a flash of red lips and the glint of green eyes, a cloud of dark hair floating tremulously in the air before she disappeared with a horrifying hiss into the spluttering fire. I knew who she was without a doubt.

"Morgan!" I screamed, "Don't take Moses with you! Please!" But nobody listened and, before I could do anything about it, both were gone.

Chapter Four

Without a second thought, I ran into the hallway where, hastily, I shrugged on my coat—barely able to fasten the buttons my hands were shaking so hard—and left the house, pulling the door closed behind me. Thankfully I had picked up my phone, so, standing stock still on the garden path, I rang Mum again. But there was still no reply, just an ongoing ringing that was beginning to drive me mad. I clicked off the call and put the phone in my coat pocket. I would have to try again later.

What had I seen in there? It was Morgan Bloom without a doubt, the woman I'd seen in my cellar, albeit in a different form, as some sort of smoky mist. But she'd taken Moses and disappeared into the fire. How could that be? It was impossible! Thank God the fire hadn't been lit properly. Otherwise, what would I find when I got back inside, the burned body of poor little Moses in the fireplace? Oh my God, it didn't bear thinking about.

To keep myself warm, I walked down the garden

path and out of the gate, glancing at the house next door as I went by, noticing the cozy, welcoming light glowing around the edges of the drawn curtains. It was cold out here, and a fine sleety rain had begun to fall, already soaking through my coat, making me shiver and rub my hands together. Hunching my shoulders, I turned up my collar, wishing I'd thought to bring a hat and gloves, or even a scarf. But the thought of going back into my lovely new home filled me with horror. And how sad was that?

Close to tears and dreading the thought of having to wander the streets until I felt ready to go home, I pushed open Mabel Montgomery's gate and walked purposefully up the garden path. She had said I could visit any day but a Tuesday, and today was Thursday. And although it would be too dark at the moment to see the pear tree in her backyard, at least I would be able to see something, and I had to admit, the possibility of company was very hard to resist.

A bright white light came on as I neared the front door, illuminating the two steps up to the porch and the neat garden laid out either side, its pocket-sized lawn speckled with fallen leaves of crimson and orange and surrounded by well stocked tidy borders. She answered on the first knock, hurrying to the door, an anxious look on her face which cleared when she saw it was me. She was dressed as before in black trousers and a fluffy red jumper, although this one had silver sprinkles around the cuffs and the neck, so she still resembled a busy little robin redbreast.

"Hello, dear. Is everything all right?" She frowned, causing a deep vee to form in the little space between her eyebrows.

"No," I shook my head. "Would you mind very much if I came in to talk? I know it's too dark to see the tree, but—"

"Of course. Come in, dear." She took my coat as we stood on the porch and hung it on an old wooden coat stand. I followed her through to the sitting room, which was similar to mine with its massive fireplace and beams that crisscrossed the ceiling, but with more furniture and more ornaments and clutter.

A coal fire burned hungrily in the grate, sending out tongues of orange flames so that the room was warm, cozy, and inviting. A large clock in a glass dome ticked loudly from its place on the mantelpiece, and the television was on, the sound muted, the flickering screen showing men wearing Stetson hats—reminding me, with a rapid beating of my heart, of my boss—hiding behind rocks and pointing guns at each other.

"Sit down, dear." She indicated the settee, and I sank down gratefully, leaning forward and putting my cold hands in front of the fire to warm them. Even though I barely knew Mabel as yet, the relief I felt at being with her was overwhelming.

"I've got something that you might like to try," she said. "I won't be a moment." She bustled off into the kitchen, of which I could see just a little from the half open door. I got an impression of lots of white—white tiles, white paintwork, and a white butler sink, a glaring white light that lit every corner. It would be from that window that the pear tree could be seen. Maybe she'd show me later.

Mabel came back carrying a bottle and two glasses, which she placed on the small occasional table situated between the settee and her chair. "Pear wine," she said with a smile whilst pouring a generous measure into each glass. She handed one to me and, inviting me to clink with hers, said, "Tally Ho!" before taking a great gulp and then licking her lips in a tiny birdlike fashion.

"Tally Ho?" I questioned as I took a sip, "Don't people usually say cheers?"

She laughed over the top of her glass, her eyes bright and beady as the little robin that she reminded me of. "Well, yes, I suppose they do. But I like to be different," she said decisively.

"Mm," I said. "Wow, this is good stuff!"

"I thought you'd like it—also made from my own pears. How did the pie go down? Did Lily Makepeace have a slice?"

"Very well, and yes, she did. In fact, everybody did. Oh, sorry, I'll bring your dish back tomorrow."

"Oh, don't worry about that, dear. There's no rush."

"What do you do at your over sixty club?" I asked her.

"Oh, all sorts of things, dear. Embroidery, a book club, a bit of light exercise, yoga, Pilates, we listen to music—a bit of everything. Why? You're far too young to join us yet!"

I laughed and said, "Yes, about thirty years too young. What does Lily Makepeace do?" I asked. "I'm just curious."

"Well, Lily's only just joined, but she set herself up straight away for the book club. She's very interested in the history of Whitby and reads about Dracula and ghosts and such things."

"Oh, maybe she knows the history of Pear Tree Cottage too."

"Hmm," Mabel replied thoughtfully. "Maybe she does." We sat quietly, sipping our wine, when she said, "Do you want to talk now? I've got to say, you've got more color in your face. When you came in earlier, you looked as white as a sheet—actually, you looked as if you'd seen a ghost."

"Well, that's the thing," I told her. "I think I have, on at least two occasions." I knew my voice was trembling, but I couldn't help it.

Taking another sip of wine, Mabel said, "What have you seen, Chrissie?"

Everything came pouring out then; the sighting of who I thought to be Morgan and Seth Bloom in the cellar, the weird hunched figure in the mirror, and now tonight, Morgan Bloom appearing as some sort of mist and taking Moses with her into the fire.

"Hmm. Rita mentioned somebody called Morgan. Don't worry. Moses will be fine. Morgan wouldn't harm her familiar."

"I hope not. I'm dreading going back indoors, scared of what I might see in the fire. Who's Rita?" I asked.

"The lady who used to live in your house, Rita Peacock."

"Oh, you mean my mum's neighbor's aunt who moved to Scotland?" Rita Peacock, an apt name. I wondered if she looked like a peacock just as Mabel was like a robin and Lily Makepeace a wren. It was all about birds. With a sinking heart, I realized that crows were also known to be witches' familiars. I hoped desperately that Morgan Bloom wouldn't bring one of those fluttering, beady eyed black creatures into the house.

"Yes, she went away very suddenly—barely said goodbye, even though we'd been quite good friends for years." She took another sip of wine. "Let me show you the pear tree, Chrissie."

Painfully, one hand on the small of her back, she got slowly to her feet, and I followed her tiny hobbling figure, eager to see the pear tree but also eager to find out what Rita Peacock's experiences with Morgan Bloom had been compared to mine. It was so comforting to know the strange things I'd seen weren't just a figment of my imagination.

It was dark in the kitchen, but Mabel didn't put on the light, just stretched up a hand and pulled back the net curtain so I could see the tree, etched black against the darkness outside, its thick knobbly branches pointing up to a sky streaked red with sunset. It was a lot taller and wider than I'd expected, taking up most of the small backyard. Mabel suddenly produced a torch and shone it at the window so that in the white circle of light, I could see its lower branches were hung with pears that wobbled in the breeze like pale little suicides. The rest of the yard was the same as mine, down to the three bins standing in a row against the wall.

"Can you see where it's grown up through the flags?" she asked as she shone the torch to the bottom of the trunk so I could see where the stone flags had been pushed up by the tree's twisted roots.

"Yes, how weird that it grows here and not in my garden, as it used to."

"I know. It just suddenly appeared right here." She switched off the torch, throwing the garden into blackness again, so we went back to the sitting room and sat by the fire that hissed and spat hot embers onto the carpet. Mabel put an old mesh fireguard in front of it and then, leaning forward with the bottle, topped up my wine. She told me then that Rita Peacock had had several encounters in her home with Morgan and Seth Bloom. "I think in the cellar, in her bedroom, and in the kitchen. She came round here a few times when it all got too much for her—just like you did tonight, I suppose."

I nodded and said, "Yes, I've got to say it's good to have your company. And to tell you the truth, I'm not looking forward to going back to my place at all."

"Don't you worry, dear." She leaned forward and patted my hand. "I'll go back in with you. A bit of moral support." She thought for a minute or two, then said, "Rita said she felt as though she was just watching their lives—you know, Morgan and Seth Bloom—but not taking an active part. She didn't think they could see her. Is that how it is for you?"

"Yes, that's how I felt when I saw them in the cellar when Morgan was holding Moses. I spoke to them, but there was no reaction. I reached out to get Moses back from her, but they disappeared."

Mabel topped up our glasses again. "Did you see the hunched figure in your own mirror? A mirror that you brought with you?"

"No, the mirror was already in the house, in the sitting room. I assume it must have belonged to Rita. Now I know why she didn't take it with her."

"Hmm, yes, I remember her saying something about

the mirror—the one hanging over the fireplace? So she didn't take it with her. Hmm."

"Thinking about it though," I said, "The hooded figure could be Morgan Bloom."

"Well, I suppose it could be, but—"

"Yes. Maybe her long black hair looked like a hood. I only had a brief glance before it disappeared."

We nodded at each other as we sipped the wine. I was feeling pleasantly drowsy and loose limbed, my head limp on the back of the settee, as the wine snaked down my throat like a beautifully scented oil. My God, it was certainly potent stuff. Cowboys thundered across the TV screen on glossy black stallions, pursued relentlessly by Indians wearing elaborate feathered headdresses.

The great domed clock on the mantelpiece had chimed ten o'clock when I finally pulled myself unsteadily to my feet. Getting back to my house was a blur, but I remember vaguely standing on the doorstep waving goodnight to Mabel after we'd poked at the cold dead fire, searching the ashes for the remains of Moses. But thank God we found nothing there. And although we called for him and looked in every room, there was no sign of the fluffy black cat.

I went to bed then and fell immediately into a deep sleep, spiraling down deeper and deeper as if into a spinning black hole. I had vivid dreams of the ghostly wraith like figures of Morgan and Seth Bloom as they reenacted their tempestuous lives, the tip tapping of a beak on the window as a fluttering shiny black crow peered in with its beady all-seeing eyes, and the frantic meowing of Moses as he materialized from the ashes of the long dead fire. Then I slept the long peaceful sleep of the dead, of the dreamless, not waking until a weak sun glowed yellow in the sky and showed its face at the window.

~*~

A sharp rat a tat at the front door made me jump, and as I was in the middle of painting my nails with a thick black polish borrowed from Layla, it certainly wasn't a good time either. Keeping low, I peered through the sitting room window, but all I could see was half a person—one leg of a skinny jean, a high heeled boot, and one arm covered in some sort of fluffy leopard print coat. Slowly, carefully opening the door—it's very difficult when your nails are wet—I peeped through the crack.

"Who is it?"

"Good God, Chrissie, it's me, your mum."

"Mum!" I flung the door open, totally shocked to see her standing there.

"Well, aren't you going to let me in? Oh my, what are you wearing?"

She stepped into the hallway trundling a tiny pink suitcase behind her as I stood there, open mouthed.

"What's up? Cat got your tongue?" she asked brightly.

The word "cat" made me think of Moses—the still missing Moses—and reminded me of the fact that ever since that night, I was still afraid, looking over my shoulder, in my own home. Suddenly I found my voice. "I've been trying to get in touch with you for ages. Why don't you answer your phone?"

"Oh, don't even go there, Chrissie. It's either been stolen, or I've lost it, I'm not sure. I suspect it was when I had too much red wine at The Lamb a couple of weeks ago, and somebody nicked it off me. You can't trust anybody these days." She stood in the sitting room doorway looking around, "Oh my God, it's like stepping back in time. Old fashioned, isn't it?" Gazing around and seeing the room with Mum's eyes, I could see what she meant. Not Mum's scene at all. Well, not now at any rate.

A bit of background. My mum had been on her own for a few years now, maybe four or five, because Dad left her for another woman. A younger woman called, wait for it, Myrtle Groves! If it had a number in front of it, it could be somebody's address. Anyway, the whole thing was all a bit much for Mum, who had always been such a devoted wife. It left her a bit…what's the word? Brittle? Although she swore she didn't care at all now, and she'd changed a lot, not only in her ways but her appearance. A total transformation from the slightly plump mousy downtrodden woman she'd been before. Even so, Mum looked alarmingly thinner than ever, making me, with my somewhat curvy body, look almost obese.

Anyway, imagine the Zandra Rhodes bob but in a blonde shade—flaxen, I think it's called—thick black eye makeup, and pale pink lipstick. Well, that was Mum's look now. And her clothes were different too. She wore skinny jeans a lot, sometimes even short skirts, with little cropped tops and high heeled boots. She was wearing the skinny jeans ensemble now, with a short furry leopard print jacket over the top. The whole look didn't go well with her name, Doreen, but I was sure if Mum had her way, she'd change that too. She looked so different now I didn't think even Dad would recognize her.

"Sit down, Mum. I'll put the kettle on, make you a cuppa."

"Thanks, love, a coffee would be great." She followed me, exclaiming over the long narrowness of the kitchen, peering from the window at the plain backyard, and then watching as I took mugs from the cupboard, got out sugar and coffee, and milk from the fridge. "Why are you dressed like an old washer woman, Chrissie?"

"Oh, thanks, Mum, I thought I looked okay." I gave her a scathing glance. "I'm a Goth," I explained. "It's the Whitby Goth weekend, and almost Halloween too, so I'm meeting up with some people from work later for a few drinks." I looked down at my long flowing black skirt, corset type top, and heavy Doc Martin boots. I was even wearing a long black wig to cover up my very un-goth-like Shirley Temple hair. "I was painting my nails when you arrived. Look." I spread out my hands to show her my shiny black nails.

"A Goth? Oh, yeah, nice. I wondered who all those crow like people hanging about at the station were. Wow," she said thoughtfully. "So that's why that bloke was wearing fishnets. I quite like your black lipstick. Can I borrow some?"

I shook my head, feeling like the adult with the child, as we went into the sitting room, me carrying a tray laden with mugs and the sugar bowl, and Mum sashaying across the room in her heels. We sat in front of the fire, sipping our drinks and inhaling the rich smell of the coffee.

"What are you doing here anyway, Mum?"

"Well, that's nice, isn't it?" she said, mock offended, "I thought you'd be pleased."

"I am," I told her. "I was worried. I've been ringing you a lot."

She frowned and said, "What for?" She leaned forward and added another spoon of sugar to her half empty mug. "I know," she said, seeing my look. "Shouldn't have too much sugar." She patted her non-existent stomach.

"Well, it was about the black cat. He's gone missing, and I wanted the contact for your neighbor's aunt." I took a gulp of coffee, but it was too hot, burning my lips and making me grimace. I waved my hand in front of my mouth.

"I told you, my neighbor's aunt said she never even had a black cat. It must have been a stray. Cats are like that. They don't always stay. If they can find somewhere better, then they're off. Selfish like that, they are."

I wished I hadn't mentioned Moses disappearing now. There was no way I was going to tell her about the strange happenings at Pear Tree Cottage. I knew I wouldn't hear the end of it if I did. And, anyway, if she had any idea that there were ghosts in this house before I could blink an eye, she'd be trundling her little case along the garden path in search of a cheap B&B. "Well, there's no reason why Moses wouldn't stay here. What's wrong with it?"

"I never said there was anything wrong with it. To tell you the truth, Chrissie, I think you've imagined the whole thing. Black cats indeed!" She took a grateful sip of coffee.

Smiling but feeling a slight twinge of impatience with her, I shook my head. "No, I didn't imagine it, Mum."

Suddenly I remembered the awful feeling of loneliness I'd had only a couple of days before, and the relief that Mum was here with me now felt so good that, putting any irritation aside, I jumped up and enveloped her in a tight hug. It was so unexpected—we've never really been that cuddly with one another—that she fell backwards into the cushions on the squashy settee.

She felt so tiny and bony compared to the squishy softness of her body from years before, but she hugged me back and said, "You don't mind if I stay for a few days, do you love?" And unusual for Mum, "I've been feeling a bit lonely back there in Leeming. Felt like I needed a break."

"Of course you can, Mum." Relief coursed through me, and the thought, *At least I won't be alone if anything ghostly happens,* went through my mind. I watched her closely, and for all her young woman's clothing and look, there were new lines around her eyes and her mouth that I'd never noticed before.

My heart ached for her until she said irritably, "I don't know how you stand the racket from those squawking seagulls, though, Chrissie. I bet they'll drive me up the wall. And the sea as well, all that shushing up onto the sand—drives me nuts!"

I shook my head, thinking of the noise she put up with all the time from the swans, ducks, and honking crazy geese that fought all the time on the reservoir in Leeming.

"Oh, by the way," she said casually as I took her upstairs, her boots clunking on each stone step, to show her the spare room. "My name's Zandra now. No more boring Doreen for me."

"Zandra?" I said. Blankly I stared at her, thinking how weird it was that this very thing had passed through my mind earlier, although I hadn't thought for one minute that she would do it.

"Changed it by deed poll," she said sweetly before trailing in with her suitcase and closing the bedroom door in my astonished face.

~*~

The Rose & Crown Pub, situated on a tiny steep back street in Whitby town center, was lit up like a Christmas tree as Mum and I walked towards it later that evening. The building, with its tiny bulbous windows and black and white exterior, looked like a relic from the days of the Tudors, and I half expected Henry the Eighth to come out of the great wide-open door carrying a foaming flagon of ale and wearing an embroidered vest and jeweled codpiece. Loud music was pumping out into the street and, mingled with the inevitable cawing of the gulls, it made for an almighty din. People looking like large scary black crows stood in the doorway smoking and drinking.

Inside, the bar was heaving with queues three deep, a lot of the women looking very similar to Morgan Bloom. But Mum, having changed into a short black dress over which she still wore her furry leopard print jacket, pushed her way to the front and quickly ordered. "Two glasses of red wine, please, and make them large ones." I'd tried to dissuade her from accompanying me, but she wouldn't hear of it. "A daughter of mine going out to the pubs on her own? You must be joking!"

"But I'm meeting friends, Mum."

The answer was still a definite no and a "What sort of mother would I be if I didn't want to meet your new friends from work?"

Hands waving in the air alerted me to Milly, Layla, and Pat, who were sitting at a table with Norman, Pete Horner, and even Lily Makepeace who, joining in the Goth type fun, wore a long black cape and red lipstick that she'd purposely let bleed a little at the corners of her mouth, so it resembled blood. Ah, Dracula and vampires! My heart beating hard, I searched the table for a Stetson hat and a loud checked overcoat, but unfortunately, my boss, Richard Curtis, wasn't there. Seriously, though, it was far better that he wasn't. Being sworn off men was extremely difficult when he was around. I noticed the pub was decorated for Halloween, all wispy cobwebs in the corners and along the bar, and creepy plastic spiders and furry bats. Ugh!

"Gordon Bennett, it's Chrissie Lewis," said Pete Horner, his sharp weasel face breaking into a grin as he stood up and made a little mock bow. He was also dressed as something resembling Dracula in the whole ensemble of high collared cape lined in red silk, beneath which I caught a glimpse of a crimson waistcoat and black trousers, his hands encased in white gloves. "And who is this vision of loveliness that you've brought with you tonight?"

Before I could reply, Mum gave a loud braying laugh and said, "Zandra, pleased to meet you," and held out a limp hand, which Pete grabbed hold of and began to shake heartily.

I cringed at her new name, wondering what she'd

do if I shouted out, "No, wait a minute. Her name's Doreen." That'd take the wind out of Pete Horner's sails a bit, wouldn't it?

"Well, I gotta say, what a doll."

"She's my mum," I told him as I sat down next to Milly and Layla and nodded to Lily Makepeace and Norman. "Everybody, this is my mum, come to visit from Leeming." They all raised their glasses and said hello, at the same time chinking against each other's glasses with a resounding "Cheers." Layla looked much the same as she did at work, and Milly looked much the same as Layla did at work. Norman, his attempt at Goth simply wearing blue jeans and a black top, the hood pulled over his head and most of his chin—to hide the acne?—sipped morosely at his pint.

Pete's expression was one of shock. "Well, I don't Adam and Eve it. Come sit next to me, Zandra. I wanna know all about you."

I turned away then and began to make conversation with Milly whilst Layla spoke to Lily Makepeace and the miserable looking Norman, still keeping an ear on Mum's conversation.

"What's your name then?" she asked as she plonked herself next to him where he sat in the corner.

"Pete," he told her, and when she looked at him questioningly, "Pete Horner."

"Oh yeah," she said, nudging him hard in the ribs

and, from the expression on his face, almost winding him. "Little Jack Horner sat in a corner." She gave another loud braying laugh before taking a big glug of wine.

"Is she really your mum?" asked Milly, whispering right in my ear.

"Yes. Why?"

"She's a one, isn't she?"

I nodded. "Yeah, you could say that. She's all right, though."

"You from London?" I heard Pete ask her.

"Ooh no, from Hampshire originally, but I've lived up here in the North for years."

"Got a pot and pan, have ya?"

"You what?"

"Pot and pan—old man?"

"Oh. I see what you mean! Thought you meant in me kitchen cupboard." Another great bout of braying donkey like laughter spouted from both of them as they moved even closer, thigh touching thigh, on the old worn seating.

Norman suddenly got up, clutching his empty pint glass. When he was far enough away, queuing at the bar, Milly, glancing over her shoulder first, turned to me and said, "What was wrong the other day, Chrissie, in the office? From the look on your face, I gather that you might have seen something in the safe room." When I didn't answer straight away, she pleaded, "Come on, Chrissie, you can tell us." By now, Lily Makepeace, Pat, and Layla were in on the conversation. "Did you see Norman take something from the petty cash tin?"

"I think I did," I whispered, and then cringed as a song by The Cure suddenly blared out from the speaker above me, and a group of Goth girls standing at the bar screamed, "Aaah! Robert Smith, I love him!"

"Yeah, we've all seen it, but we've got no proof."

"Take a picture on your phone or a film if you see anything again," said Lily in her tiny bird like twitter. "God knows, as his boss, I've tried to speak to him, but he just won't respond. Just keeps saying, "No comment, no comment," just like you see in the films."

"Yeah," put in Layla. "He can't keep getting away with it. We didn't even have enough money saved up for tonight, so God knows how much we'll have for our Christmas do."

"Whoa," said Milly suddenly, catching me in the ribs with her elbow. "Look who we've got here!" before giving me a knowing nod.

I turned around just in time to see a Stetson hat bobbing along in the crowd like the snout of a dolphin moving through water. Then, not the loud checked overcoat as I expected, but a black Gothic vampire jacket with a silver bats wing collar over snug black trousers and a black frilly shirt open at the neck, so his chest hair was clearly visible. Everybody turned to stare as he threaded his way through the tight knit throng to our table. Norman came back from the bar with his pint and, sitting down, gazed at Richard Curtis as if he was an apparition.

"Hey there." Richard nodded and, bending closer to me, said, "Hi there, Chrissie."

My heart was beating so hard I was afraid it would jump out of my throat and land, a pulsating lump, on the table between us. And what would everybody say to that? I gave a shaky nod and said quietly, "Hello, Rick."

"Hey, if it ain't Mr. Tex and his sex-o-lets," said Pete Horner in a silly sing-song voice. "I like your whistle and flute."

Rick frowned and shook his head slightly. "Whistle and what?"

"Whistle and flute—your suit."

"Oh gee, thanks, Pete. Hey, you'll have to teach me some of that old rhyming slang."

"Good God," I heard Mum say as we all gazed at my boss, hanging on to every word between him and Pete Horner, a total vision of loveliness. "What's this then—Mills & Boon? You look exactly like a hero from a romantic novel. High cheekbones, sexy green eyes, the lot." All of this followed by the loud, braying laugh.

"Well, thank you, ma'am. I'll take that as a compliment." I noticed that his face colored as he gave a slight nod of his head.

"My mum, Zandra," I said, having to say her new name almost choking me.

"Mighty pleased to meet you, Zandra," he said. "Okay, drinks all round." He gave a great wide grin showing all his lovely white teeth and then, with a wink in my direction, turned around and went to the bar.

"Good God," said Mum again, peering around Layla, her eyes as round as saucers. "Who's that, Chrissie?"

"It's my boss, Mum," I told her.

"What, Mr. Wigglesworth?" she said slyly, glancing sidelong under her lashes. "Well, I didn't expect him to look like that—and I bet you didn't either."

Everybody, even the miserable Norman, burst into hysterical laughter whilst I gave what must have passed for a watery grin and shook my head in despair.

"It's complicated, Mum," I said. "Mr. Wigglesworth was called away just as I started the job, and Mr. Curtis kindly stepped in—"

"Mr. Tex, you mean," said Pete Horner quietly, giving Mum a sideways grin.

"He's only going to be here for six months," I said. "Then he'll go back to Arizona." Loud pulsing music echoed around, making me shout.

"Arizona?" said Mum shrilly. "Don't let him go back there, Chrissie. If I was you, I'd dig my claws in and keep him right beside me. He's too much of a dish to end up alone in Arizona!"

Pete Horner butted in again. "Who said he's gonna be alone, eh, Zandra?" He nudged Mum hard with his elbow. "Girl in every port, I bet." Once again, the loud braying laughter erupted as they shifted even closer, their thighs rubbing against each other, so close Mum was almost sitting on his lap.

A hot wave of annoyance flared up in me and, with the whole table watching and listening intently, I said icily, "I'm not the type to dig my claws in, Mum. And, as I've already explained, Mr. Curtis is my boss and only my boss. Is that clear?"

"Okay, love," said Mum good naturedly. "Keep your hair on. Only having a laugh, aren't we, Pete?" She took a sip of her drink as the two of them exchanged glances and yet more braying laughter. "You've just got to forget all about that two-timing rogue back home and open yourself to something new."

Questioning eyes turned to me at the words "two-timing rogue back home," just as a tray of drinks landed on the table, glasses rattling noisily against each other. Glancing up, I met the sea-green gaze of my boss, Richard Curtis, who, after squeezing my shoulder with his large warm hand, sat down next to me and, picking up his foaming pint glass, raised it high and said, "Well, cheers everybody. Here's to letting go of the past and something new for us all!"

"Cheers," said everybody, holding their glasses in the air and clinking them against each other's, even staggering to their feet as if Richard Curtis was King Henry the Eighth himself. I gave him a grateful glance, and he smiled back, giving me a sexy wink that sent shivers hurtling down my spine. I felt weak and watery as a pint of bad beer. All the signs were there. All the cracks in the armor I'd so carefully built around me were appearing slowly but surely, and I definitely didn't need Mum to tell me to "forget about that two-timing rogue back home and open yourself to something new," because I think I already had.

Chapter Five

The sea was rough and grey, mirroring the sky, tipped with frothy white as it rolled up onto the shore. I didn't know how Mum could get irritated with that sound, the shushing as it rushed up onto the sand, taking shells and seaweed back with it into the deep dark sea. I found it relaxing, soothing even, and making me so glad that I came here to Whitby to live by the sea. Shaking my head yet again, I went over the evening before and our night out in the Rose & Crown Pub. I remembered the loud thumping music and the hot black clad bodies and the creepy spiders and bats hanging from cobwebs on the walls and the ceiling. I had a vague recollection of Mum and Pete Horner's loud braying laughter, Norman's morose face giving me sidelong contemptuous glances, and Milly, Pat, Layla, and even Lily Makepeace's infectious giggles.

I remembered the looks everybody gave us when Richard "Tex"—as Pete Horner called him—Curtis, came to sit beside me, his warm thigh pressed against mine, making my insides churn. He asked if there'd been any more ghostly happenings in my house, so of course, I told him all about Morgan Bloom appearing as some sort of a misty apparition and taking Moses with her into the smoldering fire.

"Has your cat shown up since?" he asked me.

"No," I said, shaking my head sadly. "I've no idea where he is."

I'd left Mum in bed that morning and, from the way she had staggered home last night, leaning on Pete Horner until he left us, with a very slurred "Goodnight, Zandra, Chrissie," at the gate of Pear Tree Cottage, I didn't think I would see her any time soon. "Red wine is the nectar of the gods," I remembered her saying as she swayed slowly up the stairs to her room.

Shivering with the cold, I left my seat perched on a rock in the little sandy inlet, having decided to walk back towards the town. I had a sudden urge to climb the one hundred and ninety-nine steps to the abbey. I hadn't done that yet and really wanted to see the beautiful view from the top and also have a look around inside. But as I moved away, my booted feet making soft squelching noises on the smooth sand, my surroundings began to darken at an alarming rate and, glancing up at the sky, I saw that it was no longer grey, nor even daytime, but black and sparkling with tiny stars, the glowing white moon suspended like a great globe. The sea was quiet now, the roughness of earlier replaced by a placid calm, and tiny white frills of water reached like prying fingers up onto the streaky wet sand. Gulls cawed and wheeled like drowning sailors screaming for help.

A babble of hysterical shouting came to my ears, and, squinting my eyes, I could just make out a great army of people walking onto the beach, roughly pushing a young woman in front of them. They'd tied her hands tightly behind her back, so her shoulder blades stuck out like the budding wings of an angel. She was beautiful, tall and slender, silky black hair blowing around her face in the sea breeze, her lips a blood red line, and her green eyes flashing with defiance and anger. As when I'd seen her before, she wore a long black dress with a white apron tied over the top, and because of her beauty, stood head and shoulders above the rest of the rabble, who wore rough ill-fitting dresses, tunics, or trousers, and who were rowdy, dirty, and totally deranged.

Why was this happening now? I wasn't in Pear Tree Cottage, where I'd seen Morgan Bloom before. Didn't she and her brother, Seth, haunt that place and that place only? Panicked, I spun around where I stood, scanning behind me. People had been there earlier, ordinary people walking the sands, people chattering to one another, dogs bounding, and children laughing. Now they were gone, and all that lay in front was a wide expanse of sea and sand, high rocks towering forbiddingly behind and gulls wheeling and screeching in the sky. The salty smell of the sea was all around, in the wind that pulled at my hair and slapped at my face, and in the very air I breathed.

"Witch, witch, witch," they chanted. "Kill the witch, kill the witch." Their voices echoed all around, just as eerie as the incessant crying of the gulls. With an awful sinking feeling right in the pit of my stomach, I realized this was the angry mob of villagers who had tried Morgan Bloom as a witch and, unless I ran away right now, which for some reason I was finding impossible to do, I would have to witness the drowning of an innocent woman by this unruly mob.

My heart pounding and my mouth dry as a bone, I ran towards them, shouting, "No, no! Leave her alone! No!" But nobody heard me, nobody even saw me as I ran even closer, arms flailing, my mouth opening and closing. "No, please stop, please stop! Morgan is not a witch!"

Before my astonished eyes, four of the men hoisted her between them onto their shoulders, the way pallbearers would carry a coffin, one at each shoulder and one at each foot, and began to march into the sea. Deeper and deeper they went, the waves curling around their knees, their thighs, and their chests, the sea lapping at their bearded chins. Morgan's long skirts dangled in the water as she twisted and turned within their grasp like a slippery fish, desperately trying to get away. Her screams echoed around the deserted beach.

"Unhand me, you fools!" she shouted. "Unhand me! I am no more a witch than any of you! Unhand me!" Her cries became weaker and weaker as the sea drew higher and higher, until eventually, with a shout of triumph, the four men let her go. She floated at first, and then, thrashing about, legs flailing, tried to sit up, which was even more difficult with her hands tied behind her back. I saw her face, a pale oval in the gloom, and made to run towards her, but it was too late, for she began to sink, her long dress belling out around her like a beautiful sea anemone, but pulling her down, as if chains were around her, further and further into the merciless black sea.

"Ha ha," shouted one of the women, an old hag, showing the blackened stumps of her teeth as, laughing, she ran manically along the sands towards the sea. "She's a witch, she's a witch, she floats, she floats." Others joined in taunting and jibing, running into the waves and thrashing at the water with their hands, laughing as they watched Morgan Bloom struggle in the water. The last thing I saw was her slender white hands that somehow she'd managed to untie, grasping at the air over and over, until they sank too and, with barely a ripple, she was gone.

"She sank!" I shouted at them, tears streaming down my cheeks. "She's innocent! She was never a witch—she sank!" But nobody heard me, nobody even saw me, and if they had, would they have cared? Being so bloodthirsty and hungry to kill, they would probably have drowned me too. And now Seth Bloom was there, a shocked look on his face as he gazed at the sea for a long time. But there was nothing there now, and the rabble had gone. Turning, he caught sight of me and, with a wave of his hand, began to run over.

"Surely he can't see me." I looked over my shoulder—there was nobody there, but he was obviously waving at me. He must be able to see me! What did that mean?

"Hey, Chrissie, are you okay?"

Turning my head, I came face to face with not Seth Bloom as I thought I would, but my boss, Richard Curtis, his sea-green eyes looking intently at me. He wore a dark green waterproof coat and snug black trousers, and a black bandana warmly hugged his neck. The Stetson was perched on his head, hiding his silky blond hair. Reaching out his arms, he clasped both my shoulders as if he was going to shake me and asked again, "Chrissie, are you okay?"

I couldn't believe he was there, right in front of me. I'd been thinking of him earlier before I'd seen the murder of Morgan Bloom and wondering when I'd see him again. The evening before had opened my eyes even wider to his considerable charms, which could be a dangerous thing. Boss and personal assistant is usually a no-go area for a relationship. I'd been desperate to know how he felt about me, but that was before—before Morgan's murder. I suppose I could refer to it as BMM. I was too distraught at the moment. Our budding relationship would have to take a back seat for the time being.

Cupping my hands around my mouth, I gazed at him and said, "Didn't you see it?"

Wordlessly he shook his head. "What? See what?"

Looking around, I saw that it was daytime again, the moon and the stars gone, replaced by a blue cloud speckled sky and a watery yellow sun, and people, ordinary people wearing ordinary clothes, were strolling on the sands, dogs were running about, and children squealed and screamed. I saw a man throwing a ball and his two dogs bounding happily after it, racing against each other to get to it first. There was no darkness and no unruly mob baying for Morgan Bloom's blood.

"Hey, you're shaking with cold. Come on, let me buy you a warm drink. There's a café just over there by those rocks."

With his arm firmly around my shoulders, we stumbled like drunks across the smooth sand to the café, which stood square as a box with a pointed red roof, a soft yellow light shining in the windows, looking as welcoming and comforting as an oasis in the desert. The door opened with a ping, and people looked up and idly watched us as we took a seat at a small yellow Formica-topped table. We ordered our drinks from a basic menu, coffee for Rick and hot chocolate for me. There was a man reading a newspaper sitting alone at the table next to us. The smell of fried bacon and toast hung in the air.

It was warm and steamy, the windows covered in streaky condensation. My fuddled mind almost expected to see a message, "Help me," written with Morgan Bloom's shaky finger on the glass. The coffee maker made a whooshing sound, and more steam escaped from the shiny silver machine, adding to the fug as we sat and waited, the events of earlier running through my mind. I could still see Morgan Bloom being manhandled by the unruly mob and her panicked efforts to save herself even as she was sinking like a stone to the bottom of the sea. My hands trembled as I took the mug of hot chocolate from the waitress and brought it to my lips. It was scalding hot, so hastily, I pulled it away as Rick took a sip of coffee.

"Too hot?" he asked, a small smile curving his lips, lips that were red and juicy as ripe strawberries from the cold. I gave a thin smile and nodded as he told me to blow on it. "You need a warm drink," he said to me. "You're white as a sheet. What happened out there, Chrissie?" He'd taken off his Stetson, and his hair hung soft and silky on his forehead and dangled in his eyes. He pushed it away, a gesture I was getting to know so well.

I gazed at his hat that sat between us on the table and, taking a sip of the now warm hot chocolate, I whispered, my throat feeling rough and sore, "I don't know." Tears threatened, and frantically I blinked them away, but they wouldn't go and clung stubbornly to my lashes. I was annoyed with myself for being so weak and useless.

"Hey, hey." He patted my hand reassuringly. "Don't get upset. You know you don't even have to tell me but… uh…. Well, maybe it would do you good to talk?"

Putting my mug down onto the table and taking a deep breath, I said quietly, "I think I just witnessed the drowning of Morgan Bloom as a witch. I know it's hard to believe, but it was the same as when I saw her and her brother in my cellar. But this time, right there and then on the beach, there was a great mob of people baying for her blood. She had her hands tied behind her back, although she managed to get them free, but it was too late, and she drowned. She struggled so much, though." I put my hands to my head and raked them through my hair.

I knew I was gabbling on and speaking far too fast, so I stopped for a breath, wondering what Rick could be thinking. It was all very well telling him about the weird things that had happened in my house because, yeah, right, the house could be haunted. But to see all this outside the house, on the beach—was this too much for even him to believe?

The door pinged as a small group of people came in, and automatically we turned to look as they took off their coats and, chairs scraping against the floor, sat at a table as the waitress hurried over to take their order. Rick gazed at me long and hard, frown lines in the space between his eyes, the only thing to mar his good looks.

"Wow. Are you sure?" he asked incredulously.

I nodded and said, "Yes, I'm really sure. They murdered her. Oh my God, Rick, they murdered her."

He took a sip of coffee, and I saw that his eyes widened, and he looked away, down at the table, unable to meet my gaze, it seemed. A cold shiver passed through me, and I said, "I know it's hard to believe—"

He took a deep breath. "If you saw a murder, Chrissie," he whispered, leaning towards me, his elbows on the table, "Don't you think you should go to the police?"

"Exactly," said a voice, and the man who had been sitting quietly reading his newspaper stood up and strolled over to us. "I wondered when somebody would say that." He flashed an ID card at us. "Detective Inspector Charlie Lawson, Ryedale and Whitby Police. I'm sorry, but I couldn't help overhearing your conversation. You should maybe lower your voice when you're talking about witnessing a murder."

He was very tall and thin and so pale that his shock of thick dark hair looked all wrong for him like he wore one of those curly wigs that men used to wear centuries ago. If I hadn't been so worried and scared, it would have made me laugh. His eyes, staring me down, were dark and penetrating, set deep into the sockets.

"No," I shook my head. "You don't understand. This isn't something the police can deal with." I noticed that Rick frowned at my words and gave a very slight shake of his head.

"Um, I'm sorry, miss," said the detective inspector. "But murder is definitely something the police can deal with, and if you have information that could help us, you are bound by law to come along to the station to tell us what you know."

People were beginning to turn around and stare. The detective inspector didn't seem to care that his voice was loud and echoed all around the small café.

"Are you on duty?" I asked him.

He gave a curt nod and replied, "I'm always on duty, miss."

Rick took my hand and, squeezing it reassuringly, said, "Come on, Chrissie, let's go along with the detective inspector. Just tell him what you know. There's nothing to worry about."

"Nothing to worry about at all," said the detective inspector as he held the café door open. It shut behind us with a hiss, trapping the fuggy air inside.

I noticed that he gave Rick a strange look as he placed the Stetson on his head. Outside it was cold now, the air fresh and breezy. Darkness was falling already, and the moon beginning to show its face, reminding me that winter was on its way. People still strolled on the sands in the gloom, their dogs bounding around them, and the sea roared, white tipped waves crashing onto the shore.

What have I done? I thought to myself. How would I

be able to tell the detective inspector what had happened on the beach today without him thinking I was going slightly mad, as Freddie Mercury once sang. I felt awful that Rick had gotten mixed up in this, and I'd bet anyone a fiver that he was wishing he'd never gone for a walk on the beach today, had never seen me, let alone asked me if I was okay.

"I'll go with you," said Rick as we arrived at the detective inspector's car after he'd offered to give us a lift to the station. "A bit of moral support."

Grateful for his presence, I gave him a thankful smile as we both ducked into the back seat and the detective inspector, with a reassuring nod, started up the engine. The car purred to life, reminding me of Moses and the tiny rumbling sounds he used to make when I stroked his long silky fur. His absence was just another worry. Something else for me to be anxious about.

Rick fumbled for my hand on the seat between us and squeezed it reassuringly. Absentmindedly I squeezed it back, as my heart clattered like an express train, and my breathing came short and sharp as if I was gasping for air. This time not because of the close proximity of Rick, but because of nervousness and fear. A glimpse in the driver's mirror showed my eyes tense and nervous as a cornered prey. Speeding along to the station, shops, pubs, and buildings all a blur through the window, my stomach in knots, I wondered what on earth I would tell the detective inspector when he questioned me.

Chapter Six

Mum was lounging on the settee, both hands wrapped around my "Best Girlfriend in the World" mug that Stuart had bought me many moons ago, and wearing her usual attire of skinny jeans and a tight top when at last I arrived home after a couple of hours of questioning at the station. I noticed she was wearing a full face of makeup, and big sparkly earrings drooped from her ears. I knew I would have plenty to think about later, but for now, I would have to deal with any questions Mum might have about where I'd been for most of the day. I needn't have worried.

"Hello, Chrissie, love. Had a good walk?"

I think Mum had failed to notice it was pitch black outside now, but I replied, "Lovely, thanks, Mum. You okay?"

"Couldn't be better. I'm off out in a bit."

"Oh yeah," I said, shrugging off my coat and hanging it on one of the pegs by the front door. "Where you going?"

She giggled and blushed a bit and said, "Well, Pete—you know, Pete Horner?"

"Yes, I know who Pete Horner—round the corner—is, Mum," I said as I went into the kitchen to put the kettle on.

Quick as a flash, she sprang up from the settee and trailed after me. "Well, he texted me earlier and asked if I wanted to go out for a beer tonight. So, why not, I thought!"

"Yeah, why not, Mum," I replied.

She put the "girlfriend" mug, pink lipstick marks around its edge, on the worktop. "You all right with that?"

The kettle, which was still hot from Mum's drink, bubbled ferociously to the boil. I poured the water onto a spoonful of coffee and stirred thoughtfully before saying, "Mum, you're old enough to make up your own mind, aren't you? Especially about men."

I don't know why I hadn't just said, "Yeah, okay, Mum. You go out, have a good time." Why was I being so off with her? Maybe because she was going out on a date without a care in the world, and here I was in a predicament—witnessing murders that happened hundreds of years ago, and being questioned by the police (who just happened to be in the same café at the table next to me—what are the odds on that?). And because of that, my blossoming relationship with Rick, my lovely boss, might be over before it had even started. Yeah, perhaps that was why.

"Ooh, bit snotty, aren't you?" She giggled and nudged me hard in the ribs.

I laughed and nudged her back. "No, I'm not!"

"Yes, you are!"

"No, I'm not."

"You are!" She nudged me again, hard.

"Ow! Mum, don't be so childish."

She stood there, a tiny little girl like figure, her hands on her hips, head thrust forward, and said, "Never mind, Mum, you can call me Zandra from now on."

"No way," I replied, picking up my mug and padding into the sitting room, then lowering myself gratefully onto the settee.

"Why not?" she said, trailing after me like a bad smell.

"You're my mum," I said. "That's why I call you Mum. Never mind Zandra anyway. You're Doreen!"

"How dare you?" she said, her face beet red and angry. "That's not true. Doreen is dead and gone. I'm Zandra now. A different person altogether."

"RIP, Doreen," I said sarcastically. I took a sip from my mug. It was really hot, and I winced as it burnt my tongue, which served me right.

Zipping up her boots and throwing on her little furry jacket, she grabbed her bag and said, "Just to think, before you came home, I was going to ask you to come out with us. Maybe you could hook up with that good looking boss of yours. Make up a foursome." She glanced in the mirror and pouted her lips, turned her head this way and that, and fluffed up her hair. I hoped to God she didn't see any eerie black shapes hovering about beneath the glass. That would scare her out of the house in ten seconds flat.

"I'd rather stick pins in my eyes," I told her.

"Oh, you are a funny one," she spat back at me before going out of the door and slamming it behind her.

My stomach clenched, and I felt bad then and wanted to call her back. Maybe I should confess all to her. That would explain why I'd been so awful tonight. Mind you, some of it was her fault. I mean, fancy asking her own daughter to call her by her first name. And it would have to be Zandra. I mean, Zandra. Couldn't she have picked something else? I could see her point about a name change. After all, the name Doreen wasn't exactly the sort of image that Mum wanted to project. It was not a sexy, hot babe sort of name. I could see that. But Zandra?

Anyway, I had more pressing things to think about. The two hours I'd just spent at the police station being questioned by Detective Inspector Charlie Lawson were weighing heavily on my mind, and even now, I felt stupid and foolish as I recalled the look on his face when I told him my story. I was afraid he now suspected I was either a drug addict or had serious mental health issues. Even Rick was looked on with suspicion because of his habit of wearing a Stetson hat.

"Anybody who looks and dresses just that little bit different could be suspected of being up to no good," said the detective inspector as he nodded his head sagely. "It's the same as all those Goth type people you see hanging around the pubs in town. Up to no good!"

He had gazed at us both with eyes as dark as two blackberries set deep into his pale, pinched face. The hair definitely didn't help. I desperately wanted to be silly and make comments about knotty ash and tickling sticks. I didn't know why, but great surges of laughter kept bubbling up inside me. Was I going mad? After all, my situation at the moment definitely didn't go well with laughter in any way, shape, or form. A young policewoman who had been called into the interview frantically took notes, the jottings on the pristine white pages of her notebook as black and rambling as the long wandering legs of a spider.

Interview room three was small and airless, with only one tiny window smeared with what looked like seagull droppings high up on one of the white painted walls. A large old-fashioned radiator in a putrid pale yellow clanked and hissed in the corner. A jug of water and four glasses stood on the table, and Rick, giving me one of his sexy winks, poured some for me. The detective inspector pulled a dangling cord, and a strip light buzzed on, making us all blink.

"So, just to be clear," said the detective inspector.

"And to sum up. You two are boss and personal assistant and have just started working together at Wigglesworth & Horner, Solicitors in the center of town."

We both nodded in assent.

"You," he nodded towards Rick, "Are Mr. Richard Curtis, just flown over from Arizona to take up your new post. Oh, and because you hail all the way from Arizona, you have decided it's okay to wear a Stetson hat all the time in Whitby."

"Hey," interrupted Rick. "There's no law against it, is there?"

"Hmm. No, no law against it, but combine Stetson hats with witnessing a murder, and it becomes suspicious."

"I have witnessed nothing," exclaimed Rick. "And I really don't think my Stetson hat has anything to do with being involved in a murder!"

Ignoring that, the detective inspector carried on. "You have only been working together for a couple of weeks, but you, Chrissie Lewis," he nodded towards me, "Have already confided in your boss about strange ghostly sightings in your house?"

"Yes, I have," I told him. "I needed somebody to confide in. I was scared, and talking about it with Mr. Curtis helped me a lot."

"I was pleased to be helping Miss Lewis when she was afraid in her own home," pointed out Rick. "And I told her spooky stories about Arizona to help her put things into perspective."

"Hmm. You seem to have a very 'confiding' relationship together," said the inspector darkly, "For people that have only been acquainted for a couple of weeks."

I went to open my mouth and speak up again, but suddenly thought, *What's the point? He thinks everything we say is a lie.* I let him ramble on.

He nodded his head towards me again. "Chrissie Lewis, today, 19 October, witnessed a murder on the beach of a lady called Morgan Bloom. She was tried as a witch by an unruly mob of villagers and drowned in the sea. You have also seen this lady in your house, as she broke in the other night, as a phantom (and here he put up two fingers on each hand around the word 'phantom') and stole your black cat, Moses. You have also seen her and her brother, Seth Bloom, arguing in your cellar."

His voice rising higher and higher, he suddenly stopped and sat forward, his elbows on the table in front of us. The young policewoman stopped writing for a second and stared at her notes as if she couldn't quite make out what she'd just written.

"I know it's hard to believe, but—"

"But?" he said, as he got to his feet and began to restlessly pace the room. "Oh, yes, the thing I didn't mention just then is that, according to your research, Morgan Bloom existed in the seventeenth century and has, obviously, been dead for many, many years!"

Rick turned to me and said with a cheeky grin, "You saw her in your sitting room mirror too, didn't you, Chrissie?"

I gave a small smile and said weakly, "Yes. Well, I think it was her."

"Oh!" The detective inspector gave a great huffing sigh. "You only *thought* it was her that time? What was different about that time?"

I could tell now that he was getting extremely agitated and was very likely to simply explode and blow the proverbial gasket.

"Have you seen any of these people?" he asked, turning his attention to Rick.

Rick shook his head and said, "No, but I saw Chrissie—I mean Miss Lewis—on the beach just after she'd witnessed the murder. She was very upset and assumed I'd seen it too, as it was so real. I took her to the café for a warm drink. Thought it might help to calm her down, you know?"

"Do you know?" he said, suddenly thumping his fist down onto the table, making us all jump. I noticed that the poor policewoman's pen skittered across the page, leaving shorthand type marks all over it. Hastily she put her notebook up in front of her like a shield. "I could have you two for wasting police time!"

"Hey, whoa, whoa," said Rick, putting his hands up

in front of him. "Calm down, Detective Inspector. After all, it was you who asked us in here to speak with you."

"Only because I thought you had information about a *real* murder," he replied. "Not an imagined one. Not one made up in your good lady's mind!"

"Hey, she knows what she saw," said Rick forcefully.

"Do some research, Inspector," I said tearfully. "Google Morgan Bloom, and you'll see I'm right. She was tried as a witch back in the 1700s and was drowned by an unruly mob of villagers."

A black glowering look was all I got for that comment.

He had to let us go—he had nothing to keep us there for. I slumped forward on the settee, my head in my hands as I recalled the walk back home, Rick strolling along beside me, thoughtful and quiet, his hands in the pockets of his jacket. My heart ached as I looked at his handsome profile, which seemed so stern and forbidding. He hugged me close at the garden gate, so close that I could smell his musky aftershave, which I breathed in expansively.

He spoke quietly, his American accent sexy, his breath hissing in my ear. "Hey Chrissie, stay safe and don't worry. Any problems, give me a ring. You've got my mobile number. If not, I'll see you at work on Monday."

He walked away then, a dark shape fading into the gloom, the notorious Stetson hat firmly on his head, leaving me feeling just a little bit lost and alone. Monday morning seemed a long way away. I felt slightly reassured by his parting words that I could give him a ring if needed and that he would see me at work. Although thinking about it, he probably felt he had to say that and really was sick to the back teeth of me and my unbelievable stories. If only they really were just stories.

With a sinking heart, I realized he may not want to associate with me now. After all, he had a reputation as a solicitor to consider and would no way want people to know his personal assistant was a storyteller—a liar. Or worse than that, somebody who maybe toyed with illegal substances and suffered from delusions, and had been questioned by the police. I couldn't blame him if he fled back to Arizona and insisted that Mr. Wigglesworth return to Whitby.

With all these awful thoughts running through my head, I finally went into the house, afraid of any questions that Mum—or Zandra, as she now wanted me to call her—might ask. But I was alone, yet pretty sure I'd have some apologies to make when Mum came back.

The fire had died down since I'd been sitting stock still thinking, so, taking the poker, I stirred it up a bit until red hot sparks began to fly. Then, mesmerized, I knelt on the hearth rug and stared into its depths, watching the flames twist together like gyrating dancers and feeling the heat grow more and more intense on my face.

I wondered where Mum and Pete Horner were now. Probably braying with laughter in a bar somewhere.

They certainly seemed to go well together, if only for the sense of humor. Was this a match made in heaven? If so, who would have thought it? It would hopefully be a far better match than that guy called Rolph, who she'd met on the "Plenty of Fish" dating site! Now he had been a strange one, and I was sure that if he saw him, the detective inspector would suspect he owned a Stetson hat and wore it all the time for casual walks around Leeming reservoir.

Wandering into the kitchen, I poured myself a glass of wine, from which I took a deep glug, rolling the liquid around in my mouth, savoring it and enjoying the way it made me feel so relaxed after such a trying day. I noticed that the contents of the bottle seemed to have depleted at an alarming rate, and the name "Mum" ("Zandra?)" came to mind straight away as the culprit. Opening the pantry door, I poked my head in, scanning the shelves for ideas on what I could eat for a very late tea, when I heard a tiny little squeaking sound. *A mouse* was my first panicked thought, and I quickly shut the door and backed away, almost spilling my wine in haste.

"Meow," This time, it was high-pitched and shrilling and a meow, not a squeak.

I circled around, gazing at the walls and the doors, wondering where it was coming from. *It's not a mouse,* I thought with excitement. *It's a cat*!

"Moses," I called. "Moses, where are you?"

"Meeeeoooowwww"

I flung the cellar door open, and a black shape shot out, fluffy fur standing on end and shrieking like a banshee. Bending down, I stopped the crazy black thing in its tracks and scooped Moses up into my arms. "Where have you been?" I asked as I nestled my face into him.

His soft fluffy fur smelt like flowers and not of grey ash from the fire as I had imagined it would. Had he been in the cellar the whole time? Had I imagined Morgan taking him away with her into the fire? If I'd imagined that, had I also imagined the drowning on the beach? Tears both of joy and frustration rolled down my face, wetting Moses's fur, making him struggle and jump from my embrace. He leapt up onto the settee and began turning around and around in a circle before settling down and casually beginning to clean himself, his tongue very pink against his black fur. Gazing at him fondly, I poured another glass of wine to celebrate his return and then opened the pantry door again in search of food—for both of us this time.

Chapter Seven

The weeks had flown by, all gone in a blur, a red and orange autumn ending with the smoky odor of Halloween, followed by a dark and dingy November. Now it was December and Christmas rushing upon us. Mum was coming to stay for a few days over the holiday, hoping, I think, that she could accompany me to the office Christmas "do." Her aim was to do a bit more hobnobbing with the one and only Pete Horner (up the stairs, apples and pears, trouble and strife, where's me wife)!

She went back to Leeming not long after our little disagreement. Not because of "our words," she had assured me, but because she ought to show her face around and about the village and to all the ducks and geese on the reservoir that she swore blind wouldn't be getting fed if she wasn't there. I know she's my mum, but good God, she was a strange one. She told me she was keeping in touch with "little Jack Horner," as she called him. God knows what their text messages were like—just one long "lol," I would think, as they seemed to break out in hyena like laughter every time I saw them together.

There'd been no sign of Morgan Bloom since that awful day when I saw that dirty unruly mob drowning her on the beach. Maybe that would be the end of it. I witnessed her death, so now she was gone, never to return. What of her brother, Seth, though, and the rest of the family? I supposed there would always be unanswered questions about the lives of people who lived hundreds of years ago. I looked for her, though, and sometimes woke suddenly in the middle of the night thinking there was somebody loitering in the bedroom, somebody standing in the darkness at the side of the bed. I fancied I could hear her breathing, soft and puffy, and wished she would show herself. But unfortunately (or fortunately, I'm not sure which), she never did.

Moses was still with me, though, purring on the bed or on the settee or stalking the garden like a lion and bringing home trophies of dead mice and birds. I knew he thought he was doing a good thing—he was showing his love for me, right? But I really wished he would stop. Just the other morning, I almost stepped on what looked like a giant mouse—it was twice the size of Moses himself—dead as a doornail on the floor by the side of the bed. I suspected it was a rat and shrieked so hard and so loud, I thought I may have woken the dead. (It didn't wake Morgan Bloom, though, luckily!)

My boss, the enigmatic Richard Curtis, was as friendly as ever, although maybe a little more detached, as if there were a thin glass wall between us, separating us, keeping us apart. He hadn't mentioned anything about being questioned by the police—he'd not even asked me any more details about what I actually saw. And when I tried to broach the subject, he quickly headed me off and rambled on about some work-related issue.

He very rarely instigated conversation about anything other than work now, yet I'd noticed he followed me with his sea-green eyes and, when I tried to catch his gaze, looked quickly away as if he didn't want to give away the fact that he was watching my every move. Perhaps he thought I was unstable and was looking for the next opportunity to submit me to a local "secure hospital."

I knew the change in his behavior was for the best. I'd had a feeling we were getting too close and that maybe it was "on the rebound" on my part, although there was no way in this world I thought about Stuart anymore. I didn't care now that he dumped me for another woman. In fact, I was relieved and felt sorry for her. Yes, I felt sorry for the sloe-eyed Anna, as I suspected it wouldn't be too long before boredom struck and he would replace her with another, just as he had replaced me with her. And so it goes on and on and on. I thought about what the detective inspector had said about Rick and me being "very confiding towards each other for people who had only been acquainted for a couple of weeks," and I supposed looking back on it, he was right.

Anyway, Rick had already been here for a couple of months—four more to go, and he'd be heading back to Arizona, and Mr. Wigglesworth would return to take up his post as my boss. Things should be a lot easier for me then. At least Mr. Wigglesworth didn't have penetrating sea-green eyes that I longed to gaze into and a stubbly beard that was just begging to be touched. There would be no distractions. "Yes, everything will be a lot easier for me then," I repeated to myself as, like a little girl, I fervently crossed my fingers behind my back, on both hands.

~*~

"Oh Chrissie, hoik it up a bit more. Show a bit more leg, why don't you?"

"Mum, I don't want to. I like this length!"

She caught hold of the end of my midi length black dress and pulled it up well above my knees. "See, you've got lovely legs, Chrissie, and you're only twenty- eight. Good God, when I was your age, I wore micro miniskirts and didn't I cause a sensation with my long pins on display. I tell you what, Chrissie—"

"Mum, it's okay. I'm quite happy wearing a midi length dress," I interrupted firmly. "I don't feel right if I've got everything on display." And then, thinking about what she had said, I added, "Did you really wear micro miniskirts? I never saw you wearing one when you were with Dad."

"Oh no, I didn't then. God no, he wouldn't have let me. I wore them years before I met him."

"He wouldn't let you?" I looked at Mum in amazement.

"Oh, it's a long time ago, Chrissie, and I don't want to go back there at the moment."

I nodded, understanding Mum's need for privacy, and turned back to the mirror, making sure that, even though I didn't want to display my legs, the dress was cut low enough to show a cheeky glimpse of my neckline. Umm, perhaps a bit too much, though. Modestly, I pulled it up slightly.

"No, leave that." Mum tugged at my arm. "Go on, advertise your wares, love. Let 'em see what they'll be getting. I bet that boss man of yours would love to get an eyeful."

"Mum."

I must have had my mutinous face on because she said, "Okay, I'll back off. Let's not have a bull and cow."

"What?"

"Bull and cow—a row!" A lot of braying laughter ensued, which I couldn't help but join in with.

"You're crazy, Mum," I told her.

We were getting ready for the office Christmas "do." Well, I was trying to get ready, but Mum kept interfering. I'd been standing at the mirror for ages, making sure my dress looked all right. It didn't help that I felt a bit like a heifer next to skinny Mum. Now I was touching up my makeup, messing about with my eyelashes, and pretending I was sucking a lemon whilst applying shiny blusher to my cheekbones.

Mum was dolled up to the nines, wearing a short black dress that shimmered as she moved and knee-high boots teamed with her usual short furry jacket. But, because of Christmas, she had gone the whole hog and twined lengths of tinsel in silver and gold through her hair. I watched her as she sat on the edge of the settee, sipping at a glass of red wine and trying to entice Moses to play with a length of the sparkly tinsel. He played for a while, batting and patting with his paws as she waved it in the air, so it undulated like a snake, but suddenly he seemed bored and moved away from her, laying himself down in front of the roaring fire.

I'd made a real effort with it being the first Christmas in my new home, and a Christmas tree stood in the corner, as wide as it was tall, the lower branches sticking out like a stiff petticoat. I'd covered it in a white cobwebby misty stuff, hung colorful baubles on the branches, and threaded little lantern lights among the greenery that twinkled on and off. Even Mum had remarked on the tree and said how lovely it was.

"Ooh, do you know what, Chrissie? I could just do a ruby. Must be the wine." She inspected her glass carefully.

"It's making me hungry."

I shook my head in despair. I knew full well that ruby (ruby murray) meant curry. Was she going to speak like that all the time?

"For God's sake, Mum, are you going to speak like Pete Horner all the time now? I've had enough of him shouting that rhyming slang stuff at work!"

"He's a one, isn't he? Eh, Chrissie?" She drained her glass and, nudging me in the ribs, said, "Hurry up then, are we going out or what?"

A sudden movement in the mirror caught my eye, something black in the corner. My heart seemed to do a nose dive, and my stomach clenched as I peered closer. Moses stood up and did a cat stretch, his fur looking spiky and wrong somehow.

"Look at him, look at the cat," exclaimed Mum, "He looks all spiky, like a hedgehog!"

Peering closer still to the mirror and putting out a shaky hand, I touched the black shape with a finger, expecting—what? I really didn't know. But, to my relief, the black shape was on the tip of my finger now. Smiling and shaking my head, I realized it was a speck of mascara, and not the ghost of Morgan Bloom returned to haunt me. Moses laid back down and stretched out again, basking in the heat from the fire, as if he knew all was well and there was nothing to worry about. Morgan Bloom wasn't coming to take him away any time soon.

We stepped out into the dark. It was a bitingly cold evening with not a breath of wind, the paths sparkling with frost and the sky arching above us teeming with stars, like one of Michelangelo's beautiful painted ceilings. Trees stood tall, their branches and trunks etched white against the dark, like a black and white art photo. Seagulls shrieked as they wheeled through the air, and as if from far away, I could hear the shushing of the sea as it moved up onto the sand.

Mum linked her arm through mine as we slipped and slid on the soles of our high heeled boots. "Oh, God, should have worn me crampons!" she moaned.

"I did suggest we get a taxi," I said through gritted teeth as I clung on to Mum, my very own lifebuoy, albeit a very small light one.

"Taxi!" she exclaimed. "When it's only a five minute walk down the road?"

"Yeah, but a slippery five minute walk!" I replied. Our breath came in little white puffs like speech bubbles, a bit like Batman and Robin with their "zap" and "pow."

The restaurant was busy and so warm and cozy inside as we ducked through the door and beneath the black oak beams that crisscrossed the ceiling. It was decorated like a fairy dell, with a magnificent silver Christmas tree, paper chains, and balloons. Christmas music blared from speakers set high on the wall.

Manic arm waving from Pete Horner alerted us to

our table, where a seat for Zandra, as he kept shouting, was saved for her. My seat, for some strange reason, was next to my boss, Richard Curtis. I wondered who had saved that for me and why. Millie gave me a secret smile as I took off my jacket and hung it over the back of the chair before I sat down, giving a friendly nod to everyone as I did so.

Rick poured me a glass of wine, which I sipped gratefully. He gave me one of his sexy winks, which made my heart rev up like an express train bombing along. He looked good in his dark suit, his shirt open at the neck to show a thick mat of chest hair. I'd never seen so much of him before, and, heart pounding, I carefully averted my gaze. I noticed that he didn't have his Stetson hat on, and his hair hung blond and floppy into his eyes.

The smell of succulent turkey, roast potatoes, and vegetables hung in the air, mingling with the loud chattering of so many people. I felt a bit shy and ill at ease until Rick moved his chair slightly closer and said, "You look very lovely tonight, Chrissie. Very festive." He nodded towards my dress and the tinsel Mum had made into a coronet and perched on my head.

"Thank you, Rick," I said, aware that my voice wobbled just a little bit.

Before I could speak again, Pete Horner exclaimed, "We've got some beauties around this table tonight, Tex. I mean, look at Zandra! She's a cracker." He took a huge draw on his pint of beer and put his arm possessively around Mum's shoulders. Surprisingly, Mum colored up a bit but inclined her head around the table like she was the queen of Sheba. All the women twittered gratefully when it suddenly occurred to me that somebody was missing, the empty chair next to Lily Makepeace being a dead giveaway.

"Where's Norman?"

"Oh well," said Layla with a twist to her mouth. "Didn't we say there was something about Norman?"

"Oh yes. You left early yesterday afternoon, didn't you, Chrissie?" said Millie. "So you won't know what happened."

I shook my head, mystified. I'd left a bit before finishing time yesterday because I was picking Mum up from the station.

"He only took most of our Christmas 'do' fund," she explained.

"He's a naughtya boya," said Pat in her mock Italian speak.

"We caught him this time," twittered Lily Makepeace. "I managed to get a film on my phone." She nodded her head decisively as she took a tiny bird like sip from her glass of white wine—or was it lemonade? I peered closer but couldn't be sure.

"Oh my God," I exclaimed, "What's happened to him?"

I felt a tiny stab of jealousy as I saw Milly exchange

a glance with Rick. "I'll tell you all about it on Monday," she said quietly.

"Okay," I replied, looking from Rick to Millie, wondering what the shared look had been about.

"Yes, we mustn't let it spoil our evening," said Lily as, with a most engaging smile, she raised her glass and said, "Cheers, everybody."

"Cheers!!" said everybody, raising their glasses high. I didn't think Mum and Pete Horner had even been following the conversation, but they raised their glasses anyway and chinked drunkenly with a great bellow of laughter.

"You brahms and liszt already, Zandra?" I heard him ask her.

She must have known what it meant because she said, "Not yet, but I'm getting there." Followed by even more uproarious laughter. I noticed Millie, Pat, Layla, and Lily staring at them in amazement.

"No hat tonight?" I asked brightly.

"Oh yeah, of course, I take it everywhere with me." He gave me a smile so charming it sent shivers running down my spine. "Don't worry, it's safely behind the bar." He touched the side of his nose as if he was telling me a state secret, a gesture I could imagine the crazy Pete Horner doing. "I didn't want to keep it on in here—people might think I'm up to no good!" He gave an impish grin, and I smiled at the first comment he'd made regarding the police since we'd been questioned. The food arrived, and Rick and I chatted as we ate our starter.

"Any more sightings of Morgan Bloom?" he asked as he speared a prawn and put it in his mouth. Another surprise, because he hadn't mentioned Morgan Bloom since that day either. I shook my head no and once again tried to apologize for what had happened that day.

"Hey, Chrissie," he said, laying down his fork and turning towards me. "You know what you saw. There's no reason for you to say you're sorry to me."

"I feel really stupid," I told him. "I've seen nothing since, and because Moses is back, I've been wondering if I imagined it all. Maybe I locked Moses in the cellar by mistake, and Morgan Bloom didn't take him away at all. Maybe it's all a figment of my imagination, including the scene on the beach." I pushed my plate away, unable to eat any more. "It all seemed so real, though." I took a deep glug of wine.

Rick pushed his empty plate away too and turned fully to face me. "Stop, Chrissie, you're tormenting yourself. You're not stupid, and I'll say again, you know what you saw." We stared at each other then, green eyes meeting blue. Everything seemed to fade into the background—the Christmas music, the chatter of the other diners, the people at our table—everything became muted and hazy as we stared, unable to take our gaze away from each other.

Suddenly the spell was broken by the strident voice

of Pete Horner. "Oy, Tex, another round of sherberts?" And then turning to me, he asked, "Sex-o-let, what's your poison?"

"Um," I stammered, assuming I was Tex's sex-o-let, "Red wine, please."

"We may as well have a couple of bottles of red and white," said Rick, and then hurriedly added, "For the table, of course."

The rest of the evening was a blur thanks to the red wine that snaked like smooth oil down my throat and into my stomach, where it burned like fire. Like the fire in my sitting room that roared bright red and orange up the chimney, the fire that I thought had consumed Moses and reduced him to grey ashes. I felt immersed in a blur of laughter, singing, and manic dancing with the girls, Millie, Pat, Layla and Lily, and Mum, flashing her lovely long pins at Pete Horner. Also, surprisingly, the other type of dancing, up close and personal, folded into Rick's arms as we gyrated around the dance floor, everybody clapping and cheering us on as if we were competing on *Strictly Come Dancing* for the best smooch of the year.

There were kisses at the garden gate, hot and passionate, and words whispered into my ear, mysterious words, secrets coming to light, telling me things he'd never told me before. Private things. Things that a boss shouldn't tell his personal assistant. Could we go back there now, or had we crossed the line? He kissed my neck, tiny fluttering kisses, and drunkenly my ear, and, oh yes, my mouth again, long and hard. I felt the rasp of his stubble against my cheek and the warmth of his body pressed against mine. And then there was darkness, a deep blackness, and a sinking and a sighing.

"Go on, Zandra, you better go in now. Go with your bricks and mortar. Go on!"

"You what?"

"Your bricks and mortar, your daughter."

"Oh, you are a one!"

Shrieking laughter, and then the creak of a door, the patter of footsteps, and silence.

Chapter Eight

I awoke the next morning to a banging on the door, the little brass knocker on my front door going rat a tat tat, rat a tat tat. It took a while for the sound to pierce my foggy alcohol dead brain, but eventually, I crawled from my bed and peered from the window. Was that Mabel? I could just about see the flash of a fluffy red jumper against the dark of the coming day. Screwing up my face, I glanced at my watch—six o'clock in the morning! Oh no! Rat a tat tat again and again, and then shouting through the letterbox in a surprisingly loud anxious voice for such a tiny bird like lady. "Oh, Chrissie, please come. It's Mabel."

Quickly shrugging on my dressing gown and shoving my feet into slippers, I ran down the stairs, my head banging unmercifully on each step, and went straight to the front door and, fumbling with the lock, flung it open.

"Chrissie, I'm so sorry to wake you so early, but it's gone, and I don't know what to do." Mabel was distraught, the real proper wringing of hands distraught, tears running down her soft powdery cheeks.

"Gone?" I asked, puzzled. "What's gone? Who's gone" I was finding it hard to come to terms with being woken up so abruptly, let alone having to solve some sort of complex mystery like Miss Marple.

"Oh, it's too strange to explain," she said, sniffing hard. "Please just come and look."

I followed her tiny figure down the garden path, wincing as I felt every pebble hard and uncomfortable against the soles of my slippers. I pulled my dressing gown tighter against the cold. She led me into the warmth of the hallway and into the kitchen, where she beckoned me to the window. I peered out into the early morning darkness at the small backyard, which was swept clean and tidy, and just like mine, had three bins lined up in a row—green, brown, and blue. Shaking my head, I peered harder, not knowing what I was supposed to see when, with a sinking heart, I realized what it was that had upset Mabel so much and said in shock, "The pear tree has gone!"

"Yes," said Mabel, clasping her hands tightly at her chest. "I thought I was imagining it. Oh, Chrissie, I'm so glad you can't see it either." And then, when the full realization hit her, she cupped her hands over her mouth and said, "Oh my God, the pear tree has gone!"

Without a word, we both went to the back door and carefully stepped out into the yard. The cold hit us like a wall, and I shivered and hunched my shoulders to my ears as I gazed at the blackened stump of what had been a beautiful leafy tree, its branches bowed down with the weight of its sweet, succulent pears.

"It looks as if it's been burnt," said Mabel, peering anxiously at the stump, "Who do you think did this terrible thing?"

Wordlessly I shook my head as a chill ran through me, and it wasn't just because of the cold morning air. My first thought, or hunch, was that it was connected with Morgan Bloom and the fire that had happened in my house so many years before. I found it very hard to believe that anybody real could have come along and cut down the tree without Mabel being aware of it.

We looked at each other. "It's Morgan Bloom, isn't it?" said Mabel.

"It can't be," I said, almost to myself. "I saw her die!"

"What? You saw her die?"

"Let's go inside," I said, "I've got something to tell you." I held on to Mabel's arm and helped her back inside. She felt small and frail beneath my hand.

Once inside, sitting in front of a fire that roared like a lion up the chimney, cups of coffee clasped in our cold hands, I told Mabel what I'd witnessed on the beach, the unruly mob and Morgan Bloom's panicked cries as they drowned her. I told her about my boss, Richard Curtis, turning up, who at first I thought was Seth Bloom looking for Morgan, and our subsequent questioning from the police.

"Oh my," said Mabel, "How embarrassed you must have felt at having to explain all that to a policeman!" Mabel seemed a lot calmer now, her once shaking hands holding her cup steady.

"Yes." I nodded and took a sip of the warming coffee. "A detective inspector, no less! Detective Inspector Charlie Lawson. I haven't heard from him since then, though."

"Well," she said, raising her cup to her lips and taking a tentative sip, "You didn't break any laws, so the policeman couldn't arrest you. He was obviously well aware of that. It must have been hard for him to believe, though, but you know what you saw."

"That's exactly what my boss said!"

"Hmm. He sounds like a very nice boss," said Mabel, watching me carefully.

"Um, yes, very nice." A deep blush, which Mabel must have noticed, suffused my cheeks as the evening before suddenly came into my mind, and a shiver ran through me. I hunched my shoulders almost to my ears as the shiver travelled luxuriously all the way up my spine and then into the back of my head, where I felt as if a strong, capable hand slowly massaged my scalp. Snatches of mine and Rick's drunken conversation came to mind.

"I don't know why I'm telling you this, Chrissie, but I'm divorced." "She left me." "I have two children, two girls." "Yes, my brother, Chase." I took a deep, cleansing breath, hoping it would clear my head, but the whispers wouldn't go away.

"Are you okay, Chrissie?" asked Mabel, a concerned look on her face.

"Yes," I said quickly. "Just a bit hungover, I think. It was our work's Christmas do last night."

"Oh no, that's made me feel even worse. I'm sorry I woke you. I didn't realize how early it was. I was so—well, scared," she admitted. "It's surreal, isn't it?"

"Yes, it is, very surreal. And don't worry about getting me up early. You were there for me when I got the heebee jeebies after Morgan Bloom spirited Moses away. Getting up early to help you was the least I could do." She smiled gratefully as I carried on talking, "We need to find out who cut down your tree, though. Maybe we should report it to the council?""

"Yes, I suppose that's worth a try. I'll get on to them tomorrow. They won't be open today, although why would they do that without asking my permission? And how somebody from the council could have come into the garden and cut the tree down without me seeing them is virtually impossible. I mean, I rarely go out, only to the over sixty club once a week, and my sister's on a Tuesday. There was no mess—no wood shavings on the ground, no branches left. It's all very odd, Chrissie."

"Yes," I agreed with her. "It's very strange, but there must be a rational explanation. A fully grown pear tree doesn't just disappear from somebody's garden on its own. A tree can't uproot itself and walk, can it?"

"Those Ent things can! They look like a tree, but they're not!"

"Ent things?" I said, frowning.

"Yes, in the *Lord of the Rings*. You know, the film. They fight battles and talk and everything. You must know that, Chrissie!"

Bewildered, I shook my head. "Um, no, sorry, Mabel, I don't know anything about, what did you say? Ents? Look, I'd better get home now." I glanced down at my dressing gown and pajamas. "I think I need to get dressed."

Mabel gave a small smile and said, "I know I'm grasping at straws. I know the tree couldn't have been an Ent, and yes, you're right. There must be a rational explanation. But what rational explanation is there for all the things that have happened to you lately, Chrissie? Hmm?"

To placate her, I said, "Yes, all you say is true. But that's ghostly happenings, not the disappearance of a tree! Somebody must have cut it down." Turning for the door, I suddenly remembered something, "Oh, before I forget, Mabel, I managed to get a contact number for your friend Rita Peacock, but she refused to speak to me about Pear Tree Cottage. She said she didn't want anymore to do with the cottage and that she was trying to forget all about her experiences."

Mabel shrugged and said soothingly, "Yes, I suppose I can understand Rita feeling that way." And then, with a thin smile, she said, "Oh well, at least you tried, Chrissie dear, at least you tried."

It was only seven o'clock when I finally got home, and it was still dark outside, the sun just about peeking over the horizon and lighting up the sky with a warm blood red glow. What did they say? Red sky in the morning, shepherd's warning! A warning about what, though. Ents? Trees that walked and talked all by themselves? Maybe I should watch *Lord of the Rings* and see for myself what Mabel had been going on about.

Putting a hand to my head, which was pounding viciously now, I wearily climbed the stairs and, even though I'd told Mabel I needed to get dressed, I really didn't have the energy. So I threw off my dressing gown, stepped out of my slippers, and sank thankfully onto the bed beside Moses, who was curled up amongst the duvet in a tight fluffy ball. Soothed by his purr, I slipped into a deep, dreamless sleep.

~*~

Tap tap tap, tap tap tap. Wearily I moved my head, opened and closed my eyes, stretched my arms and legs. Tap tap tap, tap tap tap. Was there something at the window? Pulling myself up onto one elbow, I gazed uncertainly around the dim room, wondering what was tapping. Tap, tap, tap, tap, tap tap. Moses still slept beside me, his tiny furry body moving up and down like a pair of bellows pushing in and out, in and out. Reluctantly I got out of bed and padded across the floor to the window, my feet sinking into the deep carpet as if into quicksand.

It's probably a pesky seagull, I thought as I flung open the curtains, blinking as weak sunlight streamed in. A large blackbird stood on the windowsill, peering through the glass with its beady black eyes, its gaze searching and its head moving in out, in out, searching for what—for me? Tap, tap, tap at the window with its beak. Skinny legs and claws peeked like twigs beneath its thick coat of shiny iridescent blue and green feathers. Feathers that looked as if they'd been doused in petrol. Tap tap tap at the window.

I saw a worm of a pink tongue as it opened its beak and said, "Hello Chrissie, remember me?" And its face became Morgan Bloom's, her beautiful soft pale skin, wide green eyes, and red painted lips, grotesque amongst the bird's coal black feathers. Chuckling manically, it fluttered its wings and, with a savage squawk, flew away. I watched it go, swirling up and up and up over the rooftops, a black silhouette against thin scattered clouds edged with gold, and then onwards towards the sighing sea.

Heart pumping and hands shaking, I quickly pulled the curtains together and took a step back, my hands to my mouth, unsure of what I'd seen. It must have been a crow. Were they, like the black cat, a witch's familiar?

I awoke sometime later, my headache gone, feeling rested and rejuvenated, until thoughts of the night before came crashing into my mind. A vague recollection of the words Rick had whispered in my ear came back to me, and the kisses we'd shared became more and more real, making me squirm and blush. I remembered his words—he thought he'd never love again, but he did, oh yes, he did. I shivered again.

Memories of the blackbird tapping at the window didn't surface until later, memories that made me stop and peer once again from the bedroom window, gazing up into the sky and wondering if it had been real or all a terrible dream. I mulled over it, again and again, recalling with a shiver Morgan Bloom's beautiful face amongst the glossy feathers of the sinister blackbird. But, unlike the missing pear tree, which I knew was true, the freakish thing I'd seen through the window, I dismissed it as just a bad dream.

~*~

Monday morning, and I was trudging to work through a thin layer of snow that coated the paths, the buildings, the grass, and the trees overnight, as if with a soft white icing. I breathed in deeply of the frosty air. It was a winter wonderland. Seagulls cawed mournfully from a morbid, dark sky. Mum could barely be roused this morning, even though I crept into her room with a big mug of steaming hot tea. "Rosie Lee," I said softly in a sort of

London barrow boy accent. "Cuppa tea, cuppa Rosie Lee."

"You're far too cheerful in the mornings, Chrissie," she whispered as, turning her face to the wall, she wrapped herself in the duvet as tight as a sausage into its skin. *Too many nights out carousing with Pete Horner don't seem to be doing her any good,* I thought as I left her with her drink rapidly cooling on the bedside cabinet.

My stomach clenched unpleasantly as the offices of Wigglesworth & Horner came into view, dreading what I would say to Rick and also what he would say to me. What if he regretted what had happened between us on Saturday evening? What if he was embarrassed and dismissive of me and, worst of all, what if he didn't want to work with me anymore? I stopped stock still in the middle of the path, my heart racing, too afraid to go through the massive oak doors into the building. Too afraid to face my own boss. People ebbing and flowing around me glared and grumbled. "Go on, love, get a move on," someone said, so hesitantly, I picked up my feet and walked inside.

Pat greeted me as enthusiastically as ever when I arrived at the reception. We exchanged a few pleasantries about how much we'd enjoyed the Christmas do before, following the sound of manic typing, I went into the office. Pete Horner was sprawled on a chair next to Milly, avidly watching her fingers as they raced across the keyboard. "Yeah, that'll do, I think. Thanks, Milly. Just sign it off, your esteemed servant, Mr.Peter Horner!" She gave him a look, and he chuckled as he dug her playfully in the ribs with his elbow. "Only kidding. Do the, yours faithfully, sincerely whatever."

Looking up, he said jovially, "Well, well, if it ain't Chrissie Lewis!" as I put my bag on the desk, shrugged off my coat, and hung it on the old wooden coat stand.

The longing to ask Pete Horner what his intentions were towards my mum was overwhelming, but I curbed the impulse and said, "Morning, Pete, morning Milly."

"Hi Chrissie," Milly replied, "How are you?" She gave me a little sideways grin under her lashes. She looked pretty with her auburn hair piled on top of her head, and the green top she wore brought out the color of her eyes.

"Fine, thanks," I replied airily as I sat down and began to fire up my computer. I thought I'd take the bull by the horns, so I dived straight in with, "Good Christmas do, wasn't it?"

"Yes, very good," replied Milly. "You and the big boss man seemed to be getting on really well."

My emails came up on the screen, and casually I began to scroll through them. "Yes," I agreed. "It's very important for a boss to have a good relationship with his staff."

Before Milly could reply to that one, Layla came through the door laden down with a monstrous pile of photocopying which, with a great effort, she lowered onto her desk. "Morning, Chrissie." She was dressed in her usual Goth like manner of long flowing skirt and top, and lipstick that shone out of her face very black and shiny.

"Morning, Layla."

Glancing out the window, I could see that it had started to snow, big fat flakes that twirled slowly in the air and began to settle on the glass like the beautiful patterns in a kaleidoscope. I felt warm and cozy, the big old-fashioned radiator belting out the heat right next to me.

"Ooh," said Layla excitedly, clapping her hands. "It's snowing. Do we get to go home early?"

"You must be joking!" said Pete Horner. "There's plenty for you to do here. And anyway, I don't think Tex will let you go home just so you can make snowmen in your back garden. No way."

"Snowmen? But what if the buses stop running?"

"Shank's Pony for you then, Layla."

Layla looked totally bewildered. "What?"

"Your own legs," I suggested. "Walk home?"

"Eh, I'm impressed with you, Chrissie Lewis. Nice one!"

"Hmm," sniffed Layla, as she turned her back and began to shuffle about with the photocopying, expertly moving piles of papers from one place to another.

The absence of Norman was glaringly obvious by his clean and tidy desk, totally cleared of all his possessions. "What's going on with Norman then?" I asked Milly. "Fill me in on what happened."

"Well, he's gone, at last. Lily caught him in the safe room again messing about with the money in the biscuit tin, but this time she managed to get a little film on her phone. And he was actually taking money out and putting it in his pockets! Caught him red handed!"

"Yeah, there wasn't much he could say to hard evidence," interrupted Pete Horner, "Glad to see the back of him, I am! We don't want no tea leaf round here."

"Tea leaf?" asked Layla.

"Tea leaf—thief!" said Pete Horner.

"Oh, yeah," she giggled.

"We took the evidence to Rick," Milly explained. "And that was it. He was dismissed straight away. As you can imagine, Norman wasn't happy."

"He swore a lot," put in Layla. "Shocked me, really. He's got a dirty mouth, you know."

"Yeah, proper smutty, the air was blue!" said Pete Horner.

"At least now we won't have to listen to that constant sniffing!" said Layla, turning her nose up in the air in disgust. "And look at all those awful screwed up tissues on his desk! Ugh!"

Nodding hard in agreement, Milly said, "Yes, you're right, Layla. A totally sniffless office now."

"Ain't no such word," said Pete Horner, "A sniffle free office sounds better."

"As if you've room to talk about words, Pete Horner,"

said Milly with a grin. "None of your old rhyming slang makes sense!"

"Clever Mike—on yer bike!" he retorted cheerfully.

She turned back to me. "Anyway, when he'd gone, we checked how much money we had, and no way was there enough for the Christmas do, so Rick paid for everything. What little money was left in the tin will go towards the next do. Don't tell Rick I told you, Chrissie. He didn't really want everybody to know he'd paid for the whole evening. And that applies to you two as well." She nodded towards Pete and Layla.

Ah, so that was what the shared look was about between Rick and Milly, I thought. *He wanted his secret to be kept fast. What a generous man he is*. "I won't say a word," I assured Milly, even though everybody knew anyway.

"Overall, you know," said Pete. "He must have taken at least a monkey. He deserved to get the boot."

"A monkey?" said Layla, looking even more bewildered than ever as she stood there, her hands on her hips. "I've never ever seen a monkey in the safe room. He took money, didn't he? Is that what you mean? Money? Not a monkey?"

That remark was met with uproarious laughter. "Aw gawd, blimey," said Pete Horner, holding his sides in mirth. "Not a cute, furry monkey, girl. A monkey is a slang term for five hundred pounds. Oh my gawd, what a laugh." He gave a great sniff and wiped beneath his eyes with the pads of his fingers.

Lily came twittering through the door, probably wondering what was causing so much laughter. "Morning all," she said with a smile. "I don't think I've ever heard so much laughter in an office on a Monday morning. It's normally all doom and gloom."

"If you heard what Layla just said, Lily," said Pete Horner, "Then I guarantee you'd find it hard not to laugh too!"

Questioningly she turned to Layla, but Layla, with a sharp, "I'm busy at the moment," turned her back and started sorting through the piles of paper on her desk.

Shrugging, Lily turned to me. "Chrissie, Rick said could you pop in and see him when you've got a minute?"

"Oh, um, thank you, Lily," I stammered. Color suffused my face. I could feel it hot and burning on my cheeks as I rose unsteadily to my feet. Trying to appear calm and casual, even though my legs felt as weak and bendy as pipe cleaners, I walked to the door, my heart pounding and my hands shaking.

Milly caught my eye and mouthed, "Good luck," and, giving her a grateful smile, I left the room and made my way along the corridor to see my boss, thanking God that at least I'd dressed nicely this morning in a black knee length form fitting dress and a smart red jacket. My face I'd made up with a slick of eye shadow and red lipstick. My hair I'd left to do its own thing, and it tumbled curly as a nineteen seventies perm to my shoulders.

I tapped lightly on the door with my knuckles and, upon hearing the answering, "Come in," I opened the door and slipped quietly inside.

Chapter Nine

Christmas came and went with barely a whisper, a very quiet one with just me and Mum at lunchtime, and a visit to Mabel (who would have been on her own) for tea, and now we were in that weird time between the big day and the New Year. That lonely time of the year with no work because the offices were closed and, for me, bad thoughts and serious misgivings were running around in my head from the last encounter with my boss, Richard Curtis. The only good thing about that meeting was that I was in control now, in the driver's seat, so to speak, and not Rick, as I'd expected to be the case because for all he'd said to me at the Christmas do I had the feeling that he was still in love with his ex, and no way did I want to lay myself open to a broken heart again. Trying a different tactic in a situation can sometimes work wonders. Although how long I could keep up this charade remained to be seen.

The smile that greeted me was both warm and charming, which threw me a little as, because of all the baggage he'd let slip on our night out, I'd been prepared for the cold shoulder treatment, the gradual pushing away. But there was no ice whatsoever in his manner, as there so definitely was outside. The whole ambience in the office was just as warm and welcoming as ever and coupled with the smell of his musky cologne, I could have been in seventh heaven if I'd wanted to be. I was pleased to see the Stetson hat and the loud checked overcoat hanging serenely from the coat stand.

"Chrissie." He padded across the room lithe as a panther and, taking my elbow in his cupped hand, escorted me to the chair opposite his desk. The chair that I always sat in when taking dictation, my pad balanced on my knee, or first thing in the morning while planning the day over coffee and biscuits. He was dressed smartly as usual in a dark grey suit and white shirt and grey tie. I thanked God that there was no chest hair on display to distract me and make me more aware than ever of his many charms. He pushed his floppy blond hair out of his green eyes as they fastened onto my blue ones. "Thanks for taking the time to see me."

I inclined my head gracefully as a queen.

The snow was falling thicker and faster now, and I could see from the window people hurrying past on the busy High Street, heads lowered as they battled against the chilly wind, their winter coats and hats flecked with thick white flakes.

"Coffee, Chrissie?" he asked, nodding towards the percolator he'd brought in from the kitchen and put on his desk, together with a bowl of sugar and milk in a jug. I nodded yes, and he handed me a mug just as I liked it, thick and black, the aroma comforting as I inhaled it deeply and took a gulp.

He sat down with his own mug in his hand and, thoughtfully stirring it, said, "I think I have some explaining to do to you, Chrissie."

"And I to you, perhaps?" I said. I felt powerful and unafraid and suddenly knew how I was going to play this situation.

Frowning, he said, "Why? Why would that be the case?"

"Well," I said carefully, "I've sworn off men for the duration, so no way should I have been kissing you on Saturday night, Christmas or not. I'm sorry."

"Oh," he replied. He looked bewildered. I didn't think for one minute he'd expected the conversation to go this way. He'd probably expected explanations as to what he'd said to me. Oh, and tears too.

"Is that because of the two-timing rogue that your mum—I mean Zandra—mentioned?" He put his mug down on the desk and, picking up a pen, began to fiddle absentmindedly with it.

Smiling as I took another sip of coffee, I said, "Yes. Mum shouldn't have said anything about that, but until

I've come to terms with it, I'm really not interested in anybody else." I leaned forward slightly and whispered, "The things we do when we've had a few drinks, eh?"

Oh, liar, liar, pants on fire, I thought to myself. I didn't give a hoot about Stuart now, but of course, Rick didn't know that, and the need to push him away before he pushed me was too overwhelming.

He grinned, his beautiful strawberry mouth turning up deliciously at the corners. The thought that I had kissed that mouth, that my lips had touched those lips, flew rapidly through my mind. "Yes, I suppose you're right. But I did let slip a couple of things about my personal life that perhaps, from what you're saying, I shouldn't have. Do you remember what I said, Chrissie?"

"Mm, vaguely," I said airily. "You said something about having been married at some point. I got the impression that it was all over, though." I took another sip of coffee, which was so thick it had the consistency of treacle. I didn't know about drinking it—I thought I needed a spoon so I could eat it.

He sat forward, his forearms on the desk. "Yes, it is over," he said gravely, and regretfully perhaps? "And has been for a long time. Did I say anything else?"

I wasn't going to tell him what he'd said about love, that he adored me, that there was nobody else in the world like me. He was worried that I would remember, so it was pretty obvious he didn't really feel that way. As Mum had always told me, "It's the drink talking, Chrissie, always the drink."

"No, I don't think so. Why?" And here, I made sure I looked wide-eyed and innocent. "What have you done? Served time in prison? Murdered somebody?" I cupped my mouth with my hands as if in desperate shock. "You didn't kill your ex-wife, did you?"

He let out a great bark of laughter. His teeth looked very straight and very white. "No, no way. Gee, Chrissie. Whatever you think I am, I'm definitely not a murderer. Hey, that's the second time lately that I've been accused of that!" referring obviously to the questioning by Detective Inspector Charlie Lawson. Standing up, he moved over to the window and gazed outside, his hands bunched deep into the pockets of his trousers. "Oh my," he said. "Look at the snow. I didn't realize. I've definitely seen nothing like this in Arizona. Now, this is a novelty."

I giggled a bit and said, "Yes, I suppose it must be. It's far too hot for snow in Arizona. Maybe you'll want to leave early so you can make a snowman in your garden. Layla was wondering if she could go home if the buses stop running."

He turned around to face me. "Yeah, of course, she can, if it gets any worse. Wow, yeah, I've never made a snowman!" He leaned forward, his hands on his desk. "Maybe you'd like to make one with me?" And when I didn't reply, he continued, "Chrissie, I—"

I didn't want to hear any more at the moment, so I butted in. "Okay then, Mr. Curtis," I said pointedly. "Maybe I could go now and get on with my work?"

With a disappointed sigh, he said, "Yes, of course, Chrissie. There's a tape with accompanying files on top of the filing cabinet if you could do that. Don't worry, it's not urgent. I know the Christmas holidays are coming up fast." And then, as if he had just heard what I'd said, he put out a hand and roughly clasped my arm. "Holy cow, Chrissie, don't call me Mr. Curtis. It's Rick!"

Ah, I thought. *Is this where the big boss man gets angry with his helpless secretary and pulls her close, and ravishes her against the office door? Isn't that what happens in all the romantic novels*? I shrank back as a spark of anger flared in his green eyes and stayed for just a moment, but then was gone as, reluctantly it seemed, he let go of my arm.

"Okay," I said lightly as, picking up the tape and files, I wandered nonchalantly from the office without once looking back.

I hadn't seen him since that day, as the office had closed for Christmas and, even though we had swapped mobile numbers at the Christmas do, there had been no contact from him, and I would certainly not be getting in touch. Without really wanting to, I'd warned Rick off, blaming my broken heart over Stuart for preventing me from any further involvement. I should feel victorious at not letting him see me as the poor little hurt girl, but how long I could carry on working for him now was hard to predict. He probably thought me cunning and conniving, playing with his emotions. Oh, why was everything such a sham?

Had I done wrong, though, in putting Rick off? After all, why was I there, in Whitby? I'd always thought it was meant to be—the job and the house had seemed to fall into place. Was Rick supposed to fall into place too? And Morgan and Seth Bloom? Was it all meant to happen? Was there a message here that I couldn't see?

Wishing I had the answers, restlessly, I moved around the house, Moses following at my heels. I didn't know about him being Morgan Bloom's familiar, but I thought he was definitely mine now. Peering from the window, I saw that without even realizing it, the day had brightened considerably, and the rain that had washed all the past week's snow and ice away had stopped, and the sun, albeit very weak, was shining a muted yellow. Thin clouds streaked the blue, and to my delight, a rainbow appeared, its colors deep and glowing. If I could somehow get to the end of that rainbow, would I find my pot of gold?

Mum had gone out again (it must be love love love) with "round the corner" Pete Horner so, after grabbing a coat and hat and pulling on a pair of gloves, I decided to go for a walk. The garden path sparkled in the sunlight, and, gazing up at the beautiful rainbow, I took a deep breath of fresh air. As I walked to the gate, I heard a tinkling sound and, looking behind me, saw that my bracelet, a little silver one that Mum had bought me for Christmas, had come off my wrist. Bending down, I picked it up and, relieved it wasn't broken, refastened it, which was when I noticed something different in the flower border.

Peering closer and pushing away weeds and dirt with my bare hands, I saw a branch about six inches tall poking up through the earth. Shuddering, I was creeped out because it looked so much like a finger, a dead person's finger, that it put me in mind of people who had been called the "dead ringers." People who had accidentally been buried alive and, on waking up six feet under, had hurriedly rung a bell inside the coffin in the hope that somebody would hear it ringing and come and save them. Once recovered and out and about again, these people would be accused of being a "dead ringer" of the person who had died. Of course, I knew this wasn't a "dead ringer," but just a budding branch pushing its way through the earth, but I did have a peculiar feeling of what it could be. Right or wrong, before I knew what I was doing, I was running up next door's garden path and knocking excitedly on Mabel's door.

She came outside with me, wrapped up warm in her long furry coat, looking like a little fluffy chick now instead of a robin and, peering down, said, "You could be right, Chrissie. If it is the pear tree, it will grow really quickly. Well, at any rate, it did when it appeared in my backyard."

"Wow." I shook my head. "Things are getting weirder than ever around here. And just to think, I wouldn't have noticed it if my bracelet hadn't fallen off."

"You'll notice it soon," said Mabel with a shudder. "If it grows as big as mine did. How extraordinary!" She shook her head as if she couldn't quite believe what she was seeing. "We'll keep an eye on it," she said, waving goodbye as I set off on my walk.

I was determined to do as I'd intended on the day I'd seen that awful baying mob drown Morgan Bloom. So, setting off at a brisk pace, I made my way to the bottom of the 199 steps. Whitby Abbey, here I come.

~*~

"Is it really you?" And when there was no reply, I heard, "Morgan?" Seth Bloom's voice sounded panicky and afraid.

"Yes," came a whispered reply. "I'm here, Seth. A little bedraggled and cold—so very, very cold. Have you seen Moses, my heart, my familiar?"

Whispered voices alerted me to the fact that somebody was there. I glanced around uneasily as I reached the top. I'd climbed the 199 steps easily, not even needing to stop and sit on the benches to catch the view. I wasn't worried, for I would be able to see the beautiful vista once I was at the top, although, surprisingly, it was growing dark now, so I'd have to be quick before it was too late. Uneasily I glanced behind me, sure that somebody was there hiding in the shadows. I could almost feel somebody breathing, gasping, a pulsing in the air, a pulsing all around me.

I stood and gazed at the magnificent view at the top. The great expanse of the sea, all the trees, houses, gardens, and street lights coming on, lighting up the roads and paths like a galaxy, so tiny from up here, like a toy town. A soft breeze tugged at my hair as if with a baby's fingers. Turning around to face the abbey, I saw that the ruin looked tall and forbidding in the half-light. But all at once, the sky darkened, and a bright moon shone, and millions of stars began to twinkle.

The air turned colder, and a chill ran through me as I saw that the abbey was a ruin no longer. It rose up in front of me as handsome and complete as it would have been many centuries before. The great doors stood wide open, and, with a weird compulsion as though a hand pushed me from behind, I walked inside. The air felt even colder, icy and damp.

The whispers began again. "I have warm blankets and spiced ale. I will make you well again, Morgan. Where are you?" A figure appeared just in front of me, and I knew just by the shape of him, his breadth and his height, even without seeing his handsome face, that it was Seth Bloom. With no surprise that I was here again, back in time, I followed him down steep stone steps and long dark, twisting corridors, the ceilings so low that I had to crouch. He walked slowly, burdened down as he was by thick blankets and a jug from which liquid splashed onto the stone floor as he moved from side to side.

Morgan's voice was nearer, although still weak, and Seth turned into a room small as a dungeon, the walls misshapen and the floor covered in straw, where she lay curled as a fetus, shivering and shaking in her sodden clothes.

"Quick, quick," said Seth as, keeping her modesty, he helped to remove her wet skirt and top and then tucked the warm blankets around her. Raising her up into his arms, he put the jug to her lips.

She swallowed and said, "Ah, that's good. Thank you, Seth." She lay down again, and I could see her heart jumping crazily beneath the thin material of her shift as she struggled to breathe. Her lips were parched and bloodless, as white as a clown's face, and the chattering of her teeth shook her body.

"Who brought you here?" he asked, "When I arrived at the beach, you'd already gone under the water and disappeared. I thought it was hopeless. Oh my God, Morgan, I thought you were dead!"

"Oh, Seth, I sank so quickly and so easily. But as soon as the mob had gone from the beach, that laughing and heckling mob," she said with disgust, "I made myself swim, even though my skirts dragged me down deeper and deeper." She took a deep breath. "I managed to drag myself onto the beach again, and a monk found me and brought me here, an old monk dressed in a brown cloth robe with a long dark beard." Her gaze seemed hazy and far away as she spoke. "I think he's afraid of me—he's heard the rumors. Anyhow, he didn't return."

"I told you, didn't I? I told you to get rid of the cat!"

"Ah, but Seth, it is said that a witch floats, but I sank! What does that tell you, eh Seth? I'm no witch! Where is he? Where is my Moses, my familiar?" Her voice was very weak now, reedy and thin.

"I don't know, Morgan," said Seth, a catch in his voice. "I really don't know." He shook his head wordlessly.

She began to sob, heart rending sobs that saddened me so. Tears, salty and burning, right at the back of my eyes, threatened to spill. I moved closer and tried to tell her that Moses was safe with me and that I loved him, but they couldn't see me. We were too far apart, centuries apart, they in the past and me in the future.

"Well, all I can suggest, love, is that you have a word with Moses, whoever he is, 'cos I've got a wife!"

A small man with a potbelly and a rather large walrus moustache that drooped alarmingly around his mouth stared indignantly at me whilst pointing to a woman who sat, red faced and breathless, on the bench at the top of the 199 steps. She glared suspiciously. Amidst my confusion, I noticed that it wasn't nighttime anymore, and the sun shone weakly from behind scattered clouds. Seagulls shrieked as they wheeled overhead.

"Oh," I stammered. "I'm so sorry. I—"

"It's all right, love." He put his hand up, palm forward. "But as I said before, go and see this Moses and get your love life sorted, but don't involve me. My wife's over there, and she don't look too pleased, you know what I mean?" He turned to the lady who was still sitting on the bench and still glaring. He inclined his head at her. "Come on, Lydia, get a move on!"

I made a hasty retreat, dodging through groups of people standing idly by the steps and, annoyingly, on the steps. I carefully made my way down, my heart thumping at the encounter with Morgan and Seth Bloom and the fact that I wanted to go back so I could find out what was happening to them, especially Morgan. And on the other hand, trying to quell the laughter that threatened to bubble up at my interaction with the little man. How strange it was that I was back in time but visible here as well. My first thought was that I must tell Rick such a brilliant story when, with a sickening feeling in my stomach, I realized I couldn't now. Not while I was having to play an "I don't care about you" game.

I'd reached the beach and strolled along, my boots sinking into the soft sand as I walked. I went closer to the sea and stood watching it, that great breadth of grey mirroring the sky tipped with a foamy white as it ebbed and flowed, pulling and pushing at pebbles and seaweed and almost wetting my boots. The sea made me think of

Morgan and her lucky escape after the drowning. But would she still live? I felt so sorry for her and the way she had been treated throughout her life. Her beauty and her liking for strange potions and spells, and even black cats, had gone so far against her.

Moses is my cat, I suddenly thought. *And that man thought he was my boyfriend or my husband*! Oh my God, how funny. I recalled what he'd said, "Get your love life sorted!" He obviously didn't realize he'd hit the nail right on the head. Oh yes, I did need to get my love life sorted.

How I wished I could tell somebody the tale, though. Maybe I could tell Mum? No, she was going back to Leeming soon and might not visit again if I told her anything about ghostly happenings, or indeed time travel. I knew what a scaredy cat she could be. I could tell Mabel, though. Why didn't I think of her straight away? She knew what had been going on. Yes, I'd call on her later this evening with a bottle of wine and tell all.

My spirits were higher than they'd been for a while. I power walked home with long bracing steps, arms pumping at my sides like pistons. As I neared the garden gate, I saw Mum and Pete Horner standing on the path, looking up at something. My mood was so good that I felt as though I could welcome Pete Horner into my house with open arms. Yes, and I'd even put the kettle on.

"Hey Mum, Pete, what are you doing?"

Mum looked at me over her shoulder, a frown on her

face, "Where did this come from, Chrissie? It wasn't here when we went out a couple of hours ago, was it, Pete?" She turned back again to look up, her neck stretched tight.

"No, you're right there, Zandra. What is this, Jack and the bloomin' beanstalk?" He stood there, his head tipped back, hands on his hips, an expression of awe on his face. Laughter bubbled up once again as I looked up and up. And my God, it had grown quickly. The pear tree, although very thin and willowy and bending slightly in the breeze, had grown to at least six feet tall. Just in a couple of hours. Was this some sort of record?

"Um, it's a pear tree," I told them. "A particularly fast-growing strain, I think."

"Oh." Mum still looked puzzled. "A pear tree, eh?"

"After all," I told them, pointing at the house, "This *is* Pear Tree Cottage."

"Well," said Pete Horner, seemingly lost for words as he and Mum, shaking their heads, continued to stare at the tree. "Can you Adam and Eve it then, Zandra?"

Chapter Ten

January, the first day back at work after the Christmas break. I'd barely slept the night before because of my panic at knowing I would see Rick the next day. I worried what I should do if I should carry on with my charade of indifference or do a u-turn and confess my great regard for him. In my sleepless tossing and turning state, I'd decided I would do neither but would just be the best personal assistant he'd ever had in his life, and for now, I would be sticking with that.

Of course, there'd been no word from him over the holidays and, although I hadn't expected contact of any kind, my revved up heart had done a disappointing nose dive every time my phone had shown a blank screen with no hopeful message icon flashing in the corner. Huh, maybe he really was a player, and at this moment was wining and dining some other poor girl and trying to sweep her off her feet as he'd almost done with me.

The beautiful oval mirror in the sitting room

showed a tired, pale face as I gazed into its hazy depths to do my makeup, but a slick of eye shadow and lipstick transformed it, and by the time I'd dressed in a bright red skirt suit I felt cheerful and up for anything Rick might throw at me. A fleck of mascara had once again gotten left behind on the mirror's shiny surface. Trapping it with my finger, I flicked it into the bin and told Morgan Bloom in no uncertain terms that I wasn't afraid of her either and that maybe next time she appeared, if she felt better, of course, we could have a little chat about Moses. So there!

Stepping out onto the garden path, I saw that the pear tree was flourishing at an alarming rate. It hadn't grown a lot taller yet, but its trunk was thickening, and tiny green buds had begun to appear on its many skinny branches. I thought the tree had spooked Mum a bit because I noticed she gave it a wide berth as she sashayed down the garden path trundling her little pink suitcase behind her when she left the day before yesterday to go back to Leeming.

"It's pretty odd that tree just appearing like that, Chrissie," she said, giving me the eye.

"You just didn't notice it, Mum," I told her. "And as I said before, it's a very fast growing strain."

Pat was her usual vibrant self as I went into reception. She looked smart wearing a midi length black skirt with a soft pink jumper cinched in tight at the waist with a thin belt, giving her a perfect hourglass figure. The smell of frying bacon and soft, warm croissants filtered through from the baker's next door, making my stomach rumble alarmingly. "Ooh, had no breakfast, Chrissie?" she asked, proffering a paper bag full of jam doughnuts.

"No, thank you, Pat." I patted my tummy. "I need to watch this!"

"Never mind watching it. You need to fill it," she said. And on seeing my face, mouth gaping open, she said, "Oh go on, Chrissie, have one for later." She wrapped a doughnut, all damp and sugary, in a napkin and pushed it into my hand, making it quite clear that no was not the answer she was looking for.

Humming, *"January, sick and tired you've been hanging on me,"* as I climbed the stairs, clutching the paper bag, I headed towards the office but, because Rick's door was open, as it usually wasn't at this time, I backtracked slightly and peered in. I was so unprepared for what I saw that I simply stood in the doorway, staring, wondering if anything would suddenly change even as I looked. Barely moving, barely breathing, I just stood there, my smart black shoes rooted into the carpet.

He looked up and met my eyes. "Hello, Chrissie."

"Mr. Wigglesworth!" I said, my heart beating so hard I thought it would come up into my throat and choke me. "What are you doing here?"

"Ah, Chrissie. Yes, it seems I've a lot of explaining to do."

I stood mute, disappointment etched on my face,

waiting for him to say something else, but he didn't.

"Well?" I asked him, "Why are you here? Where's Rick?" Tears sprang into my eyes, and my voice quavered with a panic that I couldn't really understand at the moment.

He came around from behind his desk and, gripping both my shoulders with his hands, said kindly, "Chrissie, go into the office and take off your coat and leave your bag there, and then come back in here. I'll make you a coffee." He nodded towards the percolator that so recently had been used by Rick right here in this office. "And then I'll tell you everything." And when I didn't respond, he asked, "Will you do that for me, Chrissie?"

Mutely I nodded and walked slowly to the office. Milly was already there, and as soon as she saw me jumped up and enveloped me in a crushing hug. She didn't need to speak. The expression on her face said it all.

"What's happened?" I asked her. "Do you know anything?"

"No." Sadly, she shook her head. "I know nothing, Chrissie. I'm just as surprised as you are to see Mr. Wigglesworth here this morning."

I dumped my bag on my desk and hung up my coat, "He said he's going to tell me everything," I told her, "So I'd better go in to see him."

"Okay," she replied, and as I turned to go through the door, said, "I thought things were good between you and Rick, Chrissie. I thought any time now, they're going to be a couple. Layla thought so too."

Frowning, I said, "But why would you think that? He's my boss. I—"

Milly shrugged. "Things like that happen sometimes, and you two seem to get on really well, and we know that he kissed you goodnight after the Christmas party because Pete told us. There, I've told you now!"

"That wasn't supposed to be public knowledge," I said angrily.

"You're both single, so why should there be a problem?" she retorted adamantly.

"I know we kissed," I told her. "But it's over now. I pushed him away before he could take me for a ride. I don't want to end up the hurt one again."

"Well, if it helps at all," she said, "We all think Rick is sincere and genuinely cares for you. That's what we can see. Obviously, you see him in a different way."

"Just because somebody who is under the influence of alcohol kisses you at a Christmas party, it doesn't mean they care," I said stoutly before turning on my heel and leaving the room. Heart thumping, I knocked on Rick's office door—well, Mr. Wigglesworth's again now—and when he said "come in," I turned the old wooden doorknob and stepped inside.

~*~

Mum had just rung, full of news from Leeming. She

chattered on and on for ages. "Here, you'll never guess what, Chrissie." I didn't think she expected an answer but just rattled on with her tale. "Anna has left Stuart. What do you think of that then?"

"I think," I told her, "That Anna has more sense than I credited her with."

"You're right there. Madge is really downhearted. I think she was hoping Stuart would settle down this time."

Madge was Stuart's mum and such a nice woman. She'd been on her own since Stuart's dad died five years before. Sometimes I thought I got on better with her than I did with Stuart. I could understand her being keen for Anna and Stuart to settle down. She'd wished the same for us, but, as I learned the hard way, living together was okay for Stuart, but at the hint of further commitment, such as engagement or marriage, he picked up his feet and ran for the hills. Or the Dog and Gun Inn in his case.

"I think you had a lucky escape there, Chrissie. You're far better off with that gorgeous boss man of yours."

"There's nothing going on with my boss," I said icily.

"Ah yeah, but there could be, couldn't there?"

"Oh, leave it, Mum, please!" Everything Mr. Wigglesworth had told me came crashing into my mind, and all I wanted to do was hang up on Mum and sit right there in my own sitting room in front of my own blazing fire and think about every word he'd said.

"I've got to go, Mum," I said. "I'll ring you later."

Hanging up, I stared into the fire, watching the flames flickering red and gold, thinking about everything that had happened lately—Rick, Morgan and Seth Bloom, Moses, the pear tree—all going around and around in my head, and also everything else that Mr. Wigglesworth had told me and all that happened afterwards and in between. Oh my, what a story I had to tell.

Settling back onto the settee and closing my eyes, I recalled him pouring coffee for me and handing me a mug just how I liked it, thick and black. Now how did he know that? At work, only Rick knew how I took my coffee.

"Where is he, Mr. Wigglesworth?" I asked.

He sat down comfortably in his chair and took a sip of coffee. He took a deep breath. "He's gone back to Arizona, Chrissie. One of his daughters—you did know he had daughters?"

I nodded and said, "Sort of." And then I thought, *Oh well, at least I know now why he hadn't been in touch over the Christmas holidays.*

"Well, she was rushed to hospital with appendicitis. He had to go back. He had no choice."

"Oh no!" I replied, "I hope she'll be all right! So that's the reason he went back? Not to get away from me?"

"No, of course not. I know he's extremely fond of you."

"You said you'd tell me everything." I sipped from

my mug and then put it on the desk in front of me. "That can't be all."

"Okay, then—I'm Rick's father-in-law."

I looked at him in surprise, almost choking on the coffee, and blurted out, "His father-in-law?"

He nodded. "Rick married my daughter, Lisa, ten years ago, and they have twin daughters aged nine, Vanessa and Emma. It's Emma that's in hospital."

"How did they meet?" I asked him, wondering why Mr. Wigglesworth was here and his daughter in Arizona.

"We were on holiday in Arizona—in Tucson. I was hoping at first that it would be just a holiday romance. My wife, Marcia, and I didn't like the fact that Lisa would be in a long-distance relationship. She was only eighteen when they met, and we wanted her to experience more of life before settling down. But I grew to like Rick so much, and when they married, we were over the moon. And even when they said they preferred to live in America, we thought it was just a small sacrifice for their happiness. After all, there's holidays and so many ways and means for keeping in contact these days, what with emails, Facetime, Zoom, text messages." He counted them off on his fingers one by one. "And then, of course, the girls came along, and that was the icing on the cake."

I nodded avidly, waiting for him to carry on. He stood up and walked backwards and forwards, his hands in his pockets. He gazed from the window and then came to sit on the edge of the desk fussily, pulling his trousers up at the knees.

"Well, my daughter decided she wasn't happy with Rick and left him for another man. Marcia and I were devastated."

"She obviously took the children with her?"

"Yes. Rick was left to grieve alone at home while Lisa took the girls to live with her new boyfriend. It was a very trying time, as you can imagine, Chrissie."

There was a pattering on the windowpane, and little droplets ran down the glass like so many tears. The wind seemed to have picked up, and the trees along the High Street began to bend and dip as if they were dancing.

"Did you know who she ran away with? Did Rick know him?"

"Yes, unfortunately," replied Mr. Wigglesworth, pausing as if for effect. "The man in question is Chase, Rick's brother. So as you can imagine, Chrissie, that really did make the situation even worse than ever."

"Oh, Mr. Wigglesworth," I said, putting my hands to my face. "That's awful."

He smiled ruefully. "Yes, it hasn't been easy, I've got to say. It's very difficult for my heart to remain with my daughter when I see how badly she's hurt Rick. And Marcia feels exactly the same as I do."

"But he only had good things to say about his brother," I remarked. "He's cat sitting for him, isn't he?"

"No." Mr. Wigglesworth shook his head. "They haven't spoken since it happened. Marcia and I have been looking after his cats. We've been over there in Arizona, you see, living in Rick's place while he came here. It's beautiful out there at the moment, Chrissie, but very hot. Unbearable to sit in, in fact."

I barely heard what he was saying as, with a pang, I recalled what Rick had said about his brother. I could almost hear his voice speaking to me, so close, his breath hissing in my ear. *"He's got a wife and two kids, two dogs, and two cats of his own, but he still offered to take my boys in. He's a great guy."* Even then, he wanted to believe everything was right between him and his brother.

Tears welled up, and with a sympathetic glance, Mr. Wigglesworth offered me a tissue from the box he kept on his desk. I dabbed at my eyes, hoping my mascara hadn't run and that I didn't bear any resemblance whatsoever to that seventies rock star, Alice Cooper. "Thank you, Mr. Wigglesworth." There was a short silence before I blurted out, "But why did he come here? What was the purpose?"

"Well, Chrissie, this is where, unfortunately, I've involved you."

"Involved me? How could you possibly do that?"

He didn't reply and, peering beyond him at the window, I saw that suddenly it was dark outside and blackness stood hard at the window, a pale moon riding high. Somebody laughed, a beautiful tinkle of a laugh, and said, "Who on earth is Mr. Wigglesworth? There's nobody here by that name. Now put out your hand, girl, let me see your palm." Glancing up from the old scarred wooden table at which I now sat, I looked straight into the haughty green gaze of Morgan Bloom.

Chapter Eleven

Obediently I proffered my palm, and Morgan Bloom grabbed my arm and pulled it towards her, regardless, it seemed, of whether it hurt me or not. Looking down at myself, I saw that I wore similar clothes to hers, although not quite as clean, for the apron was soiled with rusty stains and the dress thin and wearing into holes. I was aware that I wore a bonnet on my head and strange wooden clogs on my feet. I couldn't believe that this time they were able to see me and talk to me and that they were living, breathing, real people.

Disorientated, I wasn't sure where I was at first, but then, with a dawning realization, I knew I was in the kitchen of Pear Tree Cottage. My very own house that was now so changed, I barely recognized it. If I was able to peer through the window into the garden, I was sure I would see the pear tree flourishing, its branches hung with succulent fruit.

I took a tentative glance around. Over a blazing fire

hung a massive black cauldron, tongues of orange and yellow flame curling around its sides, the contents bubbling and filling the air with the smell of rabbit, perhaps, or some sort of bird, something rich like pheasant or duck. The scrubbed stone floor was covered in sweet smelling rushes, and even though it was daytime and a band of golden light streamed through the one tiny window, candles flickered on what looked like a deep wooden sideboard.

"You shouldn't be doing this, Morgan." Seth Bloom suddenly appeared at my side, his handsome face grave. "If anybody sees you—"

"What do I care?" she replied. "I'm doing nothing wrong." She studied my palm closely and began running the tip of her finger across the lines and muttering to herself. "Hmm, the head line, the heart line. Now this one? The life line—"

"You are too careless," he said, and then, roughly grabbing my shoulders, said, "You ever speak of this outside these four walls, girl, and I'll make you sorry. Do you understand?"

Shaking and shying away from him, intimidated by his sheer presence and good looks that were not even marred by the mole that grew beneath his left eye. I nodded my head and whispered, "Yes, sir, I understand."

"Leave her alone," said Morgan. "Can't you see you're frightening her to death? What's your name, girl?" She glanced up at me and, thoughtfully tapping her finger against her lip, said, "You look familiar." She moved her head from side to side, studying me from all angles.

"Chrissie," I whispered.

"Do I know you?"

"No, Miss. I've never seen you before in my life."

"Ah, that's good. You keep to that story, and all will be well. You don't know me. You've never seen me before in your life and perhaps never will again."

I nodded.

"You kidnapped this girl," whispered Seth. "Plucked her from the street. She's not frightened of me but of you."

"I need to practice my skill on the palm," said Morgan lightly. "I will not harm her. I just want to look at her palm. I have read yours, Seth, and many others. There is nothing new to read on them." She bent her head over my hand again so that her beautiful hair cascaded down her back and across her shoulders like a long veil of black silk. It smelt of some sort of scented oil, light and fragrant as shady woods in spring. "Hmm. Well, it seems that somebody loves you." She gazed at me with what seemed like admiration in her beautiful eyes. I started at her words and tried to pull my hand away, but she held on tight, her grip strong. "Why do you pull away? Don't you want to know?"

Not knowing what to say, I remained silent, so she carried on speaking.

"Somebody from far and away across the seas,

the Americas, perhaps? What do you know about this, Chrissie?"

Adamantly shaking my head, I said, "I know nothing of anyone from the Americas, Miss."

There was a sudden tiny squeak, and a black fluffy kitten jumped up onto Morgan's lap. She petted it with her long fingers, lovingly stroking its fur. "Ah, Moses, my dear one." Bending her head, she lightly caressed the top of its head with her lips.

Why, it's Moses, I thought, M*y Moses*. I gave a small smile, which Morgan saw as she looked up from her petting of the cat.

"Why do you smile, girl?"

"The cat is pretty, Miss," I replied.

"Yes, this is Moses. He is my heart." Her long fingers still caressed his fur as she bent her head again to study my palm. "I see a man. He looks strange, for he wears a tall hat and a long coat of check in colors so bright—I think?" Her beautiful face looked puzzled and then lightened again as she said, "He is very handsome. His smile shows teeth so white. You are lucky, girl. I would like such a man."

I smiled, although careful not to show it to Morgan, at her description of what could only be my boss, Richard Curtis. I thought of the first time I'd met him, my first day at my new job. How he'd stood with his hands cradling his hips, wearing the Stetson hat and loud grey and yellow checked overcoat, or long coat of check, as Morgan had just said. I recalled Mum's words, *"What is this, Mills & Boon? You look like a hero from a romantic novel!"* Oh, and he did, he really did. And with a sudden gut-wrenching pain, it hit me, the realization that I missed him so much and that nothing else mattered. I had to see him again. Even If it was only one more time. One more? Could I be content with that?

"Stop this now, Morgan," interrupted Seth. "Stop all this nonsense. You will turn her head." His strange yellow eyes glowed like two lanterns in his face, making me shiver.

"I only tell what I see," she replied, putting stress on each word as she spoke.

"You will be drowned as a witch," he said softly. "If you do not stop this!" He changed tack then and said softer still as, gently, he patted her shoulder. "And I say this, Morgan, only because I care."

But she didn't seem to hear and retaliated hotly. "I'm no witch!" she replied savagely. She gave him a look of such evil that her face seemed to change before my very eyes. It became grotesque and ugly, like the face I'd seen peering from the black feathers of the crow. With a jerk she pulled my hands closer, wrenching my shoulders. I winced, but she paid no heed. Giving me a sideways glance with slitted green eyes, her face smooth again, she said, "He loves you. You are lucky, but you must find him—that is your quest."

All at once, there was a rushing as if a strong wind carried me forward and a blinding light and panicky voices. I opened my eyes.

"Chrissie? Chrissie?" I looked up to see Mr. Wigglesworth looking down on me, his face so wavering and distorted that I couldn't tell what expression he wore. With effort, I tried to sit up, and immediately he ran to the door and shouted, "Milly? Layla? Lily? Anybody, please help."

There was a thundering of feet and a blur of helping hands and concerned voices, and then I was sitting on a chair, and a glass of water was being thrust into my hand. Gratefully I took a sip as the voices carried on around me. "Are you okay, Chrissie?" "Oh my God, what happened?" "She just suddenly fainted, fell down flat on her back. It all happened so quickly." "She doesn't seem to be hurt." "No, I don't think she is, just seems a bit woozy."

Everything around me slowly started to clear as if I'd been looking through a steamed-up window, and I was back in Rick's office—well, Mr. Wigglesworth's office now, I thought with a sinking heart. The beautiful Morgan and Seth Bloom had disappeared back into that other world. The concerned faces all around me touched my heart, and before I could stem the flow, I burst into noisy sobs. Such heartfelt tears poured from my eyes like a tap turned on.

There was a lot of back patting and oohing and aahing, and then Lily's voice. "It's okay, everybody, leave me with Chrissie. Will? Perhaps I could borrow your office for a while?"

"Of yes, of course, Lily, no problem."

Will? I thought. *Mr. Wigglesworth is called Will Wigglesworth?* Laughter started to replace the tears and, using the scrunched-up tissue from earlier as well as my fingertips, I scrubbed at my face.

She put a comforting arm around my shoulder and said, "Calm down, Chrissie, I think I can help." She'd pulled a chair up close to me and, handing me a clean tissue, said, "Is this something to do with Morgan and Seth Bloom?"

"How do you know about them?" I asked her.

"I was quite friendly with Rita Peacock," she replied. "The lady who lived in your house before you moved in?"

"Yes," I said, nodding my head. "Mabel told me about her, that she disappeared to Scotland quite quickly, without a word. I contacted her recently, but she didn't want to talk about anything to do with the cottage."

"I'm not surprised. She was afraid of the goings on in Pear Tree Cottage. I offered to do a cleansing for her, but she refused that too. She said it would do no good. She doesn't believe in that sort of thing she said."

"A cleansing?" I asked, puzzled, "Do you mean to rid the house of evil spirits?"

Lily nodded, "Yes."

"But I don't think Morgan is evil!"

"No, not evil, but lost, perhaps? I've always had

an interest in lost spirits. People that die but don't know they're dead. They cling to this world, not realizing they're frightening the living. Simply not knowing they should be gone."

I gazed at Lily's kindly face, surrounded by her iron-grey hair that looked so much like a cottage loaf that I wanted to cut a slice and eat it warm and buttered. She wore her usual sensible outfit of a tweed skirt suit with a high buttoned frilly blouse and flat shiny brown brogues. She certainly didn't look like a spiritual gypsy type person, who I imagined would look similar to Angela Jolie as *Maleficent, Mistress of Evil* or even, I supposed, like Morgan Bloom herself.

Lightly she patted my hand and said, "Think about it, Chrissie, and let me know if you want me to come visit you. Since I joined the over sixty club with Mabel and was put in charge of the library, I've been studying the occult, even more, especially concerning the history of Whitby and Dracula and, of course, Pear Tree Cottage. And I'm very familiar with prayers and rituals for house cleansings. Now maybe we should give Will his office back. And maybe you should go home and rest?"

"Yes," I said. "I'll think about it, thank you, Lily," I rose unsteadily to my feet, dizziness overcoming me, so I had to put a hand to my head. "I'd rather stay here, though. I'm sure Mr. Wigglesworth will have work for me to do, and quite honestly. I don't relish the thought of sitting at home alone. I'd rather be busy here."

She nodded, agreeing with me, and followed me through to the main office where Milly and Layla were busy working but looked up, concerned, as we appeared. "Are you okay?" they asked as I sat down at my desk.

I nodded thankfully, and Lily said, "She wants to stay here, so keep an eye on her, won't you?" They both nodded, and she turned to me, "I'll get Will to find you some work, okay?"

I nodded and turned to the screen of the computer while Layla said, "I'll go make some coffees. Fancy one, Chrissie?"

"Oh, yes, please," I replied.

Milly caught my eye as Layla strode from the room, her long black skirt swinging around her ankles. "Are you truly okay now, Chrissie?"

"Yes," I assured her. "I feel much better. Maybe I'm just a bit tired?" I busily started scrolling through my emails when I had a sudden thought. "I didn't know that Mr. Wigglesworth is called Will."

"Oh yes," said Milly. "Mr. William Wigglesworth. Cool name, eh?"

As we giggled like naughty schoolgirls, my phone pinged, and a text message popped up onto the screen. Staring closely, I saw with a jolting shock that the message was from Rick. My heart beating as hard as Roger Taylor beating a drum, I began to read.

Chrissie, maybe this message is a mistake, but I have to tell you that the distance between us is killing me and, now my daughter is well again, I must return to sort things out with you. I know you still hurt from your ex, but please tell me, Chrissie, is there any hope for me for the future? Rick x

Yes, yes, yes, ran through my mind as, without a thought about Milly and what she would think, my heart singing, I rose from my chair and almost ran to Mr. Wigglesworth's office to show him the message.

~*~

Pannet Park was beautiful today, even though it was January, and we were still supposedly in the throes of winter. The sun was shining in a beautiful blue sky where hazy clouds floated alongside those noisy squawking seagulls. I saw one tottering on its little legs and shamelessly begging from an elderly couple sitting on a bench, wrapped up warm in thick coats and hats, trying to eat their fish and chip lunch. Snow drops valiantly pushed their way through iron hard earth, and even the daffodils were starting to bud, for I could see a vague yellow outline beneath their lush green stems.

Hands pushed into the pockets of my coat, I strode along, the cold air nipping my cheeks red and a gentle breeze playing with the ends of my hair like tiny searching fingers. The joy I'd felt on receiving Rick's text message was still with me, and my heart rose as I walked and as I recalled Mr. Wigglesworth's pleased expression as I read the text to him. He'd been putting tapes and files into a small pile, obviously organizing some work for me at Lily's request, when I barged in unannounced.

"What were you going to tell me before I fainted, Mr. Wigglesworth?" I asked him. "You said you'd involved me somehow with your plans for Rick?"

"Yes," he told me. "When you came for the interview, I liked you immediately, and— Well, to tell you the truth, Chrissie, I...." He hesitated and restlessly stood up and, hands thrust in his pockets, began to pace up and down the room.

"Go on," I urged him.

He stopped pacing and stared straight into my eyes. "I set you up with Rick, I suppose. I felt sure you could be good together—you could help him to get over his hurt. So I arranged for Rick to come over here and for me to go over there." And when I remained silent, he said, "There, I've told you, you have every right to be extremely angry with me."

"Did Rick know about the setup?" I asked him.

"No." He shook his head. "I told him I wanted an extended holiday in America and appealed to him to give an old man a bit of a break." He gave a charming grin, not looking at all old. "He said yes immediately, as I knew he would. He was ready to get away for a while from the situation, but of course, at first, was reluctant to leave his daughters. But the thought of six months where he didn't have to pretend all was well, perhaps even be a different person for a while, was, I think for him, extremely tempting."

Sitting down on a bench now, my hands thrust in my pockets, I thought about how shocked I'd been at Mr. Wigglesworth's actions at first. But then, really thinking about it, I could see how much he cared for Rick and thought he was doing the right thing. Looking back, I remembered the rest of our conversation.

"But how did you know I was free, that I didn't have a boyfriend?"

"Well, yes, that was a tough one. But I guessed from your job application, your urge to move away from your home town, your single status, and, well, the rest was a shot in the dark, a gamble, you might say." I remembered how he'd gazed at me hopefully here, his eyes a very deep brown. "I think my gamble may have paid off?"

"Hmm, maybe," I replied.

"I have a question for you, Chrissie," Mr. Wigglesworth said. "Why did you tell Rick that you were still upset over your ex? In fact, are you?"

"How do you know about that?" I asked him. "That was supposed to be just between me and Rick!"

"I'm not sure he has anybody else to confide in, and after the way my daughter hurt him, I think he's afraid of becoming involved with anyone again. And, Rick and I— Well, we've always gotten along. And don't forget,

Chrissie, men don't always talk about such things. They tend to keep things to themselves, however right or wrong that is."

"I know," I said with a small smile. "I remember my mum saying that about my dad, and they're divorced! But I feel the same. I'm afraid of being hurt again. I felt I needed to protect myself, I suppose, so I told him I was still getting over Stuart, my ex. I'm not, by the way. I've no feelings for him now, but Rick came on so strong at the Christmas do that I wondered if he was a bit of a player, and I didn't want him to think I was becoming fond of him if he didn't feel the same way."

"I see. So both of you were fleeing from broken hearts. But finally, Rick has given in. He must know it's time to move on from the Lisa and Chase scenario, don't you think?"

"Yes, perhaps, although it seems to me that Rick and I have been at cross purposes, doesn't it, Mr. Wigglesworth? Or both on the rebound?"

"Yes, my dear, maybe so." He gave me a look from the tail of his eye and said, "So you're not angry with me, Chrissie?"

I shook my head. "No," I told him. "I don't think I am. As long as Rick never finds out you set him up on some sort of weird blind date!"

"He'll never find out," Mr. Wigglesworth assured me. "When's he coming back? Have you been in touch again?"

"Yes," I replied. "He'll be back in about two weeks. Hasn't he told you that yet?"

"No, not yet," said Mr. Wigglesworth. "But he will. I'd better start packing again, hadn't I?"

Chapter Twelve

"Yoo hoo, yoo hoo, Chrissie. It's me, Mum. Can you let me in? It's raining men—I mean cats and dogs, out here." This was followed by bellowing laughter and the clacking sound of the letterbox going back into place. Peering from the window, I noticed a taxi setting off from outside the house, teeming rain clearly visible in its headlights, and just one side of Mum standing on the porch wearing her usual outfit of skinny jeans and boots, but with a longer furry leopard print jacket that reached her knees. Her hair looked stylish in her usual Zandra Rhodes bob. Oh no, I had Lily Makepeace and Mabel coming around very soon to do the house cleansing. Could we still do it with Mum here?

Rushing to the door, I flung it open, and she sashayed into the hallway, trundling her tiny pink suitcase behind her.

"Hello, Mum, what are you doing here?"

"Oh well, thank you, Chrissie. Pleased to see me, are

you?"

"Of course I am, just surprised, that's all."

"Yeah, well, I wanted to surprise you, love. You know, those dull winter evenings—boring, ain't they? I thought we'd be company for each other—until that boss man of yours comes back, of course!" I tried to hide a smile, but Mum saw it. "He is coming back, isn't he?"

"Yes," I nodded, still smiling. "Within a couple of weeks."

"Oh, Chrissie." Unusual for Mum, she flung her arms around me and pulled me close, her wet coat soaking me through. "I knew you sounded happier last time we spoke on the phone. I hope now you can put that useless article in Leeming out of your thoughts and be happy with— what does Pete call him? Tex?" She giggled like a girl.

"His name's Rick, Mum, and I haven't thought about that useless article in Leeming, if you mean Stuart, that is, for ages. Anyone is welcome to him now."

"I don't think anyone wants him," replied Mum dismissively. "That Anna's taken off, and Madge is at her wit's end. He keeps going around to her for his meals now—and for his washing!" She shrugged off her furry coat and, draping it over the settee, made her way into the kitchen and put the kettle on. "You don't mind if I make myself at home, do you, love?"

I shook my head. "No, it's fine, Mum. Thing is,

though, I've got somebody coming round," I checked my watch, "In a few minutes time."

She gave me a look.

"Not a bloke, Mum," I said, scandalized as I watched her searching the cupboard for a suitable mug and eventually taking one with a picture of Donny Osmond on it.

"Ooh, I used to love him," she said fondly. And then, "I should hope not," as the kettle bubbled to the boil, and she poured the water over a spoonful of coffee and several sugars. "You'll definitely have enough to contend with when your boss man comes back."

How come she's still so thin? I thought as I saw her spooning what looked like a two-pound bag of sugar into her mug. "Lily Makepeace from work and Mabel from next door are coming round."

"Oh yeah? Oh, I do like that Mabel. Chirpy little woman, isn't she? And she certainly looked after us on Christmas Day." She settled comfortably onto the settee, put her mug on the little side table, and stretched her arms toward the fire. "Oh, I do love this fire, Chrissie. Miss it, I do, when I'm not here."

Well, there was nothing else for it, I'd have to tell her. I sat down on the armchair opposite her and, leaning forward, said, "Look, I'll come clean with you, Mum, so to speak. They're coming to do a house cleanse."

"Your house don't need cleaning," she said

indignantly. "It's so spick and span, I can see my face in your kitchen floor."

"Not that sort of cleaning! I've had some strange happenings. They're going to say cleansing prayers and things like that."

"What sort of strange happenings?" she said, frowning, "Ghosts and stuff?"

"Well, yeah. I didn't want to tell you before because I was worried you wouldn't stay here again, and I don't want you going to a B&B. I like you staying here."

"Ah, do you? That's nice." She took a sip of coffee and winced, saying, "Ugh, maybe I went a bit mad on the sugar."

"You can go out if you like, Mum. You don't have to be here when they come."

"No, it's okay. I'll stay." And then very decisively, "Do you think I'd leave a daughter of mine in a house full of ghosts? No way!"

There was a tiny bird like tapping and, on opening the door, Lily and Mabel twittered their way in, saying, "Hello, Chrissie. Oh, hello there, Zandra. How nice to see you."

Mum stood gracefully and inclined her head. "Likewise, Mabel. Ooh, I don't think I've met you, Lily."

"Lily Makepeace," she said, shaking Mum's hand.

"Pleased to meet you," they all twittered. "Filthy night, isn't it? Raining hard out there now," whilst taking off their coats and hanging them neatly on the coat pegs. Lily carried what looked like a large black leather medical bag with a broad silver clasp. I noticed that Mum gave Lily's tweed outfit a bit of an up and down look. Maybe reminding her too much of her old self, Doreen?

"Coffee all round then?" asked Mum as she disappeared into the kitchen, coming back a few minutes later with a tray containing the sugar bowl, milk jug, and spoons. She disappeared again, and I heard the kettle bubbling to the boil.

"Does your mother know what's going on?" asked Lily, clutching the large bag to her chest as she sank deeply into the settee, her little legs sticking up like a tortoise on its back.

"Yes," I told them. "I've just explained that I've had some strange happenings, and you've come to do cleansing prayers and to bless this house."

"*Bless this House,*" said Mabel. "Ooh, do you remember that program, Lily?"

"Ooh, I do. Sid James, wasn't it?"

"Yeah, oh so funny. And his wife, very attractive—what was her name?"

"Diana Coupland?" said Mum as she came in carrying mugs for Lily and Mabel like the hostess with the mostest.

They'd lost me, totally, all three of them. I must have looked suitably bewildered because Mabel said, "Take no notice of us, Chrissie. Just a program that used to be on the telly back in the day. You're too young to remember it."

"But anyway, enough of that," said Lily. "Let us proceed to really bless this house. Oh, before I forget, Chrissie, Mabel has just told me all about the pear tree. I've seen it in your garden. It seems to be growing very fast."

"Yes, it certainly is," I said. "A very strange thing to happen." I shook my head in bewilderment.

"I told her the Council said it wasn't them that cut it down," put in Mabel. "They knew nothing about it and said they would never go into a private garden and remove a tree. Gave me a bit of a dressing down for even thinking they would do such a thing, I can tell you! But I do miss it in my backyard."

"I knew there was something weird about that pear tree just appearing like that!" said Mum. "You mean it used to be in your yard, Mabel?"

Cringing, Mabel nodded and mouthed, "Sorry."

Turning to me, Mum said, "You told me porkies, Chrissie!"

"Only because I didn't want to scare you, Mum."

"She's only trying to protect you, Zandra," said Lily. "Now, come on, let's get on with this. There's nothing we can do about the pear tree now."

"Well, hopefully, we can still make pear wine regardless of where the tree is?" asked Mabel hopefully.

"Of course, Mabel," I assured her. "That goes

without saying."

Lily cleared her throat impressively and pulled a few sheets of paper covered in scribbled writing from the bag, and placed them on the settee beside her. She then removed a tall figure of Jesus, which she placed on the coffee table, a picture of angels floating about in the sky, and some incense sticks that she lit from the fire and wafted around the room before placing them in a little glass vase that also came out of the bag. They smelled sweet and yummy, like the inside of one of those old fashioned sweet shops.

"Is that Mary Poppins's bag?" I asked, which set everybody off with twittering and baying laughter. A menagerie in my sitting room? Whatever next.

"We have to open a couple of windows, Chrissie," said Lily, "So that the negative energy has somewhere to escape to." Obediently I opened the two little top windows and lit two big fat white candles, which had also appeared from the bag, and placed them in the candle holders on the mantelpiece. I glanced at Mum, who was sitting stock still and staring. I didn't know if she realized her hands were in prayer position, but she looked very pious and a lot more like Doreen than Zandra, which I didn't think she'd be very happy about.

"Salt," said Lily, waving a packet in the air. "This needs to be sprinkled in the entrance area."

"Why's that?" asked Mum. And when Lily gave her a bit of a look, said hurriedly, "I'm just curious like!"

"It keeps the spirits away."

"What spirits? Gin? Whiskey? Rum?" Mum cackled like a witch, reminding me of Morgan Bloom and her struggles as she was drowned by the baying mob. A shiver hurtled down the length of my spine.

"Not alcoholic spirits," said Lily smoothly. "Ghostly spirits, Zandra, ghostly spirits."

I noticed that Mabel hid a smile behind her mug as she took a big gulp of coffee. Lily gave me the packet of salt, which I duly sprinkled in the entranceway.

"Hmm, I think we're ready to begin now, ladies." She glanced around and then said, "Oh no, the lights. Please turn them off, Chrissie." I jumped up and flicked the light switch, plunging the room into darkness except for the flickering of the candles, which made the corners look sinister and creepy and dark enough for something horrible to be hiding in their depths.

"Hmm, that's better. So let us pray. Please close your eyes." Dutifully we all put our hands into prayer position, bowed our heads, and closed our eyes. "Please repeat after me. '*Our Father, who art in Heaven*'" We repeated each line after Lily like a group of nuns praying in a church, pews hard as nails beneath their knees.

The mirror glowed from the wall, reminding me of the hooded figure I'd seen there such a long time ago now. Peering through the slit of one eye, I saw that Mum was glancing furtively around the room. She looked like a deer panicking in bright headlights as she repeated after Lily, *"Forever and ever, Amen."*

Lily droned on. "I ask that you surround the entire home with an orb of light. I ask that anything inside of this orb that is not in alignment with unconditional love or that does not have the highest interest of humanity and all beings *be* released into the light of the divine.

"Thank you, angels, for filling the entire home with light. Flow light into every corner, crevice, and cabinet. Under and around the furniture, clothes, and belongings. Under the floors, in between the walls, and above the roof. Cleanse the energy and elevate the vibration. Above, below, behind, beside, and all around."

I zoned out a little bit (my mind straying to Morgan and Seth Bloom and then worrying that Moses would be okay locked in my bedroom out of harm's way) and caught up with them at, *"...vibration in the way that will most serve us and the highest and greatest good of all. I ask this according to divine will. Thank you for your support and love and frequency, and so it is. Thank you. Thank you. Thank you."*

Mum seemed to be shivering or shaking. I wasn't sure if in fear or laughter. Laughter, most likely, her shoulders were quivering so much.

Lily started speaking again with much gesticulation of her arms this time, like somebody at a presidential rally. "And I now ask you, Morgan Bloom, and you, Seth Bloom, to leave Pear Tree Cottage, to leave this life and go into the light. Amen."

Everybody repeated amen, and there was a silence, a deep dark silence, where nobody spoke, and nobody moved. The little clock on the mantelpiece ticked the minutes away, tiny weeny little ticks into the silence. The smell of the incense was too sweet now, far too sweet, and my head began to hurt, to pulse like strong fingers were squeezing and squeezing.

There was a sudden shift in the room and a tensing in the air, and the candles that were burning so beautifully flickered and died with a tiny plume of smoke so that the room dropped into darkness, a darkness so deep that, even with the light from the fire, we could barely see each other. A wind began to blow, strong and violent, and a gauzy mist appeared, twirling and whirling like a tornado.

Manic laughter rang out, and then we saw her, Morgan Bloom, within the mist, dark hair blowing, green eyes shining, and bright red lips curled into a terrible smile, reminding me of the other time she appeared and stole Moses away from me. Her voice was harsh and mocking. "No prayer or potion will banish me! I am far too strong for you!"

"Link hands and repeat these words after me," instructed Lily. Stretching out our arms, we linked hands and repeated after Lily. *"The Lord is my shepherd, I shall not want. He maketh me lie down in green pastures."*

We carried on chanting, and slowly the wind

dropped, the mist faded away, and the candles miraculously flickered to life, and even though the incense still burned, my headache eased away as if by magic. The very air felt light and not harsh and oppressive as if the spell had been broken. Morgan Bloom was gone. She was wrong. We were stronger than her.

We crumpled onto the settee, all four of us, sated, totally empty, and weak. "Good God," said Mum. "I don't believe what I saw! Do you think she's gone now? Oh my, I'm still shaking." She held out her hands, which looked like two pale, quivering fish.

"Oh, I do hope so," said Lily. She reached for her bag and pulled out a bottle. "Pear wine, anybody?"

"I'm so glad we brought the wine with us, Lily," said Mabel. "It will really hit the spot now." She put a shaking hand to her heart.

"I'll get some glasses," I said.

We'd taken our first sip when there was a terrible banging on the front door, an incessant banging that seemed to make the whole house shake. A voice rang out, high pitched and screaming, "Let me in, it's me, Morgan Bloom."

"Oh, God no," screeched Mum. "She's come back!" Even Lily and Mabel moved together in fright.

A sudden burst of bravery overcame me, and I rushed to the door and flung it open. Pete Horner stood there, suppressing a grin as he saw what must have been my terrified face.

"Ey up, Chrissie Lewis. Is Zandra there?"

"Why you, you…." I was lost for words.

"Gawd, blimey, Chrissie Lewis, you should see your boat race!"

I slammed the door in his face. "You bottle and glass," I shouted through the letterbox.

"Good one, Chrissie Lewis, you're catching on fast. I'm really proud of you! Is Zandra there, though?"

Chapter Thirteen

A hot shaft of disappointment ran through me as I reread the text message I'd just received from Rick. *Chrissie, as much as I'm longing to come back to England to talk with you and sort things out between us, Emma says she still wants her dad with her after the operation. I gotta say, I was tickled pink when she said that. Another week should have her back on her feet. Please wait for me? Rick x*

Gazing from the office window, conflicting emotions rose up in me. On the one hand, I was happy that the relationship with his daughter was so good that she wanted him with her. But on the other hand, I had worrying thoughts that he may decide to stay in Arizona for good because he couldn't bear to leave his daughters again, and a further worry that, if he saw Lisa with Chase, all the old feelings he had about the two of them might return to plague him.

Thinking about it, though, at least while he was in America, he had the opportunity to salvage the relationship with his brother. That was if it could be salvaged, of course. But from what I gathered from Mr. Wigglesworth, they hadn't even spoken since everything blew up in Rick's face, so reconciliation did seem highly unlikely. Even so, my heart sank at the thought of a further week before I could see him again before I could hear his lovely Texan drawl or gaze into his sea-green eyes and watch him impatiently push that infuriating lock of blond hair from his forehead.

I felt weak at the knees at the very thought of him. How had I allowed myself to feel this way? I'd sworn blind that I'd never become involved with a man again, not after Stuart. Obviously, I hadn't been banking on meeting anybody like Richard Curtis. Even the thought of that awful grey and yellow checked overcoat couldn't put me off him, and I longed for him to be back here where he belonged. The future was now spread out before me full of happiness and promise, just like the view from the top of the 199 steps, which was a pleasant change after being full of gloom and despair for so long.

There'd been so sign of Morgan or Seth Bloom since the night Lily had carried out the house cleanse. And what an experience that had been. I thought Mum was still in a state of shock at what had actually happened and had only stayed for a few more days after the event.

"Don't you worry, though," she assured me as she trundled her little suitcase along the garden path. "I'll be back!"

"Who do you think you are?" I asked with a grin. "Arnold Schwarzenegger?"

She gave a great bray of laughter as she ducked down beneath the spreading branches of the pear tree. "Really, Chrissie, you need to cut these branches back a bit."

Lily's voice brought me out of my reverie. "Hi, Chrissie. Do you mind if we spend a few minutes doing the advert for the new PA? You did say you'd have a bit of free time this afternoon. But if you want me to come back later?" Since Norman had gone, I'd been helping Lily out, which made me realize how stupid Norman had been to lose his job. Lily was a great boss. Not that I wanted to replace Rick, though—no way!

"No, now is fine, Lily." I put my phone back in my bag, thinking I would message Rick when I got home. "Please sit down." I jumped up and pulled a chair over for her. "Now then, how would you like to word it?"

"Well, how about something like this." She consulted her notes. "Shall I dictate?"

"Yes, please," I replied.

"Well, here goes then. Wigglesworth & Horner are looking to appoint a personal assistant to provide direct support to the company's matrimonial solicitor, Lily Makepeace. The post holder will provide comprehensive secretarial and administrative service to ensure the smooth operation of the company. They will be responsible for managing Mrs. Makepeace's diary and arranging meetings, including preparation and circulation of papers, minute taking, and follow-up work. The post holder will also take on general administrative duties to support Mrs. Makepeace and other managers as required." She stopped speaking and asked, "What do you think so far, Chrissie?"

"Fantastic. I'm sure we'll get somebody really good with an advert like this."

"Oy," said Pete Horner, who was as usual lounging in the chair next to Milly, arms up and palms cradling his head. "Don't forget to put at the end of the advert, and here I quote, 'We don't want no tea leaves this time!'" Followed by the inevitable bray of laughter.

Lily raised her eyebrows at me and Milly and, turning to Pete Horner, said, "Really, Peter, I think we've had enough of your caustic comments, for the time being, thank you very much."

"Oh, come on, Lily," he said. "You know I'm only having a bit of fun!"

"Hmm," she said whilst turning her nose up in the air. "That's debatable."

"Yeah, leave them alone, Pete," said Milly, giving him a sharp elbow in the ribs.

Grimacing and rubbing his ribs, he said, "Oy, watch out, Milly; that hurt!"

"Ooh, you baby. Serves you right," she retorted spitefully.

"I agree with Lily," I said, joining in the fun. "We had enough of you taking the mickey the other night!"

"Gawd blimey, Chrissie Lewis, you were meddling with a slice of toast!"

"What?"

"A ghost—toast!"

"What we were doing is far too complex for you, Peter," said Lily. "So we won't bother to explain. If you could please let us get on with our work?"

"Oh, I can't compete with you women." He rose lazily from his chair, patting his stomach. "I'm Hank Marvin, going for me lunch."

"Hank Marvin, starving, I suppose?" I said, grinning as he left the room.

"Chrissie Lewis, I'm getting more and more proud of you," he exclaimed, poking his head around the door.

"Oh, go away," said Milly, laughing and shaking her fist at him.

I thought about this as I walked home from work that evening, smiling to myself and thinking how lucky I was to have such a good job with such nice people, and even though I would miss Mr. Wigglesworth when he returned to Arizona next week, obviously I would be over the moon to see Rick again.

Just think, I thought. *This time next week we should be together*! Busily I began to put together in my mind what I would say to Rick in my returning text message, something like this. *Hi Rick, glad that Emma is feeling better, but also happy that she wants you to be with her. Yes, I'll wait for you.*

Let me know as soon as you get back x

Yes, that would be okay—caring but not clingy, happy for him, and looking forward to seeing him when he got back. Perfect. Little did I know then that I would never actually get around to sending Rick that text message.

Taking a deep breath, I filled my lungs with the salty Whitby air as I walked. In the distance, there was the sound of the sea as it ebbed and flowed spitting pebbles and shells onto the sand, and from above the plaintive cry of the seagulls as they swooped and dived. It was just starting to get dark, and a glowing moon hung like a lantern in the sky, and stars twinkled prettily. A plane flew overhead, its red lights blinking.

Happily, I walked up the garden path, ducking automatically beneath the overhanging branches of the pear tree. As Mum had said, I really must get them cut back. Suddenly standing stock still on the path and turning slowly around, I realized there were no overhanging branches and, with a sinking heart, that there was no pear tree either. What was it with this pear tree? One minute it's there. The next minute it's not!

Hands cupped around my mouth, I glanced down at what was left of it, just a small, still smoldering, blackened stump. Everything around it was untouched—the moist, dark earth, pale, delicate snowdrops valiantly pushing their way up to the light, leafy bushes, and budding leaves. Only the pear tree was gone, obliterated, it seemed, by fire.

The interesting reading about the burning of Pear Tree Cottage loomed heavy in my mind.

My first instinct was to call for Mabel. She understood about the strange things that had been happening with the pear tree. But just as I was about to dash up her garden path, I noticed that no lights shone a warm and comforting glow, and every window was a black hole in the face of the house. Yet even as I looked, an orange light appeared in the hall window as if by magic. An automatic light that came on when Mabel wasn't at home. After all, it was Tuesday, and she would be visiting her sister in Scarborough.

With a heavy heart, I knew I would have to go into my house alone. Fear gripped me ice cold at the back of my neck as, taking a deep breath and going resolutely towards the front door, I inserted the key in the lock and, with a shaky hand, pushed it open. The hallway was warm, the central heating humming a welcome and Moses running from the sitting room, meowing his greeting. I picked him up and cuddled him closely, so close that I could feel his purr reverberating through his tiny furry body. *Everything seems to be okay*, I thought with relief. *All nice and normal.*

I inhaled Moses's sweet scent whilst shrugging off my coat and took him into the kitchen, where he devoured his food as if he'd been starving for a year. I then moved around downstairs, putting on all the lights so everything shone bright and there were no creepy dark corners where anybody (or indeed anything) could be hiding. I lit the fire and coaxed it until it was all red and yellow flame roaring like a lion up the chimney. I pondered what had happened to the pear tree, how so suddenly the beautiful flourishing tree had become a blackened stump. I decided to put it out of my mind until Mabel came home until I heard her tip-tapping step on the garden path and saw bright lights shining from her windows.

Feeling a lot happier and relaxed and wondering why I'd been so afraid earlier, I poured a glass of wine and, taking grateful sips, wondered what I could have for tea. The sudden urge for a curry—or a ruby murray, as Mum called it—overcame me, and ringing for a take-away to be delivered seemed like a good idea. Sitting down on the settee, I reached for my phone and began to scroll through the list of local curry houses, Moses now lounging beside me, sated and happy after his food, licking his fur into place with his tiny rough tongue, the sound like sandpaper rubbing against wood.

Using my phone, I looked through the menu. "Hmm, what should I have? Biryani? Dopiaza? Masala? Korma? So many different things to choose from. What do I fancy?"

I was so immersed in what I was doing that at first, I didn't hear anything. I didn't hear the soft empty sobbing that began to fill the house, the heartfelt sobbing that I suddenly felt pulsing all the way through my body. Moses, his fur spiked in terror, his tail a bristly brush, jumped from the settee and fled up the stairs into the black hole of the landing and the bedrooms. Rooted to the spot, I wrapped my arms tightly around my body, trying to stop myself from shaking. I didn't know how much more of this I could take.

Closing my eyes, I prayed, muttering to myself, "Please God, help me. By all that is holy, help me." But the sobbing carried on and on and, when I cautiously opened my eyes, my house was different again, back to its original state, and Seth Bloom sat at the kitchen table, hunched over, his head in his hands, and it was he who was sobbing as if his heart would break into a million pieces. Two people sat with him, an elderly couple, grey haired and stooped, who I assumed were his parents, Ingrid and Asa Bloom. I could see that the woman had been a beauty in her day, just like her daughter. There was no sign of the bewitching Morgan. The black cauldron still bubbled over a raging fire, its contents weaving a rich aromatic aroma around the house. I kept myself well back, hidden in a dark corner by the wooden sideboard where candles burned fitfully.

"Oh Ma, I did my best, but I couldn't save her." He shook his head helplessly from side to side." I couldn't save her."

I felt as if I could cry with him as the woman rubbed his back with her rough work worn hands, the fingers arthritic and clenched like claws, tears running unheeded down her lined face. "I know, my boy, I know. But she was a headstrong girl and too beautiful for her own good."

"We warned her," said the old man bitterly. "She flaunted her black cat and her potions and the large blackbird that tapped its beak on her bedroom window. I heard her in conversation with that bird speaking the same as I would speak with you!"

"Stop it, Asa, stop it! Do not speak ill of our girl. She was good at heart and was at one with animals. She had an affinity—she loved Moses and the blackbird."

The old man stood up and began to stomp around the room, his heavy boots trailing mud and grime. "She was too fond of the men. She fed them potions to make them love her and read the lines of their palms for gold."

I wanted to interrupt him then and say, "No, she had a gift, a precious gift. A gift that would be understood and applauded today!" After all, she could tell from just one reading of my palm that somewhere, someday, there was a man from the Americas wearing a long coat of check. Oh, if only they could hear me.

At least Seth agreed with me, for he said, "No, they needed no potion to love her—they loved her anyway. Not just because she was beautiful, and in spite of the fact that she was willful and, as Ma said, headstrong too."

"She was evil," shouted Asa, thumping his fist onto the table, making them all jump. Ingrid put a shaking hand to her mouth. "Evil! She was a witch and died as a witch, a fate she deserved!"

"No," wailed Ingrid. "No, Asa, you have it all wrong. You did not know the heart of gold that beat within her breast. She was a good girl." She dabbed at her eyes with her apron and, turning to Seth, asked, "Where is she, Seth?"

"In the abbey, in a dungeon down deep within the earth. She was soaked through and freezing from the sea. I covered her in blankets and gave her spiced ale and the warmth of my body. I thought she would survive, but none of it did any good, and she breathed her last lying in my arms." He burst into a fresh spate of sobbing. "Oh, Ma, afterwards, I wrapped her body warm within the blankets and closed her eyes with my own hands. She was more than a sister to me. She was everything—friend, confidant, and the bravest person I ever knew."

"We must fetch her home," said Ingrid, glancing at Asa, but he was gone from her side and stood at the tiny window, peering out, his back stooped.

"What is it?" cried Seth, rushing to stand behind his father, "What is it, Pa?"

"I heard a noise," he snorted, his voice gruff. "It is the baying mob, intent on killing us too, I suppose. I see Saul there, and John, and Jordan, men who used to stand beside me. Even the women are there—Mary and Esther, Sarah too. They were our friends, and now our foe?" And then he said with venom, "We can blame Morgan for this!"

Ingrid joined the two of them at the window as I

did, hovering in the background, glad that I couldn't be seen. But yes, it was the same mob that killed Morgan, that awful rabble that had held her down in the sea until she drowned. They were holding burning tapers high in the air and chanting, "Kill them, kill them, kill them." I saw that they'd already destroyed the pear tree, and it burned now in a great pyramid like a bonfire on Guy Fawkes Night.

"No, I'll never blame Morgan," whispered Seth, glaring at his father. "Never!"

"Forget who is to blame. It is too late for that," sighed Ingrid as she looked her husband in the eye, her tears drying into snail like marks on her cheeks, "What do we do now, Asa? How can we make this better? Do you think we should speak with them? Ask for mercy?"

"No," interrupted Seth. "That mob has no mercy. You would be wasting your time. Look what they did to Morgan!"

"I will defend you both as best I can," Asa replied quietly, taking his wife's hand gently in his.

"Yes," said Seth, looking hard at his parents. "That is all anybody could ever do."

Chapter Fourteen

Thoughts of Rick ran through my mind as I peered through the tiny bulbous kitchen window with Seth, Ingrid, and Asa, at the unruly mob outside. I knew it wasn't just show with them. I had seen what the mob could do—if they wanted blood, they would take that blood and more if they desired. Morgan's family should fear for their lives. I felt genuine sorrow at Morgan Bloom's death, and her father's attitude towards her both confused and astounded me. Did she know her father had felt this way about her? Did she know he agreed with the mob that she was a witch and should die? Sorrow—I felt such genuine sorrow for poor Seth and Ingrid who mourned her so.

A strong fear overcame me as I wondered what would happen if they set the house on fire. Would I die too? Would I perish in the fire and never see Rick again? Hot tears threatened at the back of my eyes, and I wanted to flee, but where would I go? Was it best that I stay right here in the kitchen and burn with the house or run into the garden straight into the evil arms of the mob? I suspected they would put me on top of the remains of the pear tree as their very own Guy Fawkes. I remembered what I'd read about the deaths of the Bloom family and that, after Morgan was drowned as a witch, the rest of the family died in the fire. But had they? No bodies had ever been found. Was I just about to find out what really happened?"

"Quickly, Seth," instructed Asa. "Arm yourself." He threw him a dangerous looking catapult, and Seth put his homemade bow and arrow in a quiver on his back, and I saw him hurriedly place a sharp knife in the pocket of his jerkin. They packed hunks of bread and cheese and a flagon of wine into Ingrid's bag. All three of them donned heavy cloaks buttoned to the neck, Ingrid looking tiny and defenseless next to the height and breadth of the two men. Although Asa, an old man, looked less fit and agile than Seth.

"We will fight with hands and fists if we need to," said Seth. "But not you, Ma. Stay close to me and Pa. We will protect you." I saw worry etched on their faces as, sweeping through a doorway in what appeared to be a tiny scullery, we lifted the latch on the old wooden back door and left the house.

There was no backyard with its high wall and bins lined up, green brown and blue, but just a narrow rutted track leading to fields and woods that lay black as a silhouette against the navy of the sky. The moon, seemingly huge enough to step onto, hung before us, and stars shone like chips of ice. The air was cold, and I shivered in my simple black dress and apron, for I hadn't the warmth of a cloak as they had. An owl hooted, and gulls chattered like old men, and the sea still shushed white tipped up onto the shore.

"Where is the mob then?" asked Ingrid with a quiver in her voice. "They may be in the woods, waiting to spring at us!"

Seth gave a short laugh. "They may be, Ma, but at the moment, they're all at the front of the house. They are such fools. Come, let us make our escape."

"We must make haste," said Asa as he took his wife's arm with a strong grip, hurrying her along. I held back, feeling that I must stay at the house if I was to see Rick again. I watched them go, three black shapes blending into the dark woods, running fast along the stony path, so close together they seemed as one like a three headed lumbering monster. The rabble continued to chant their terrible words at the front of the house.

Ingrid looked around at the last moment, for I saw her face, a pale oval in the darkness. She raised a hand, and I glanced around, panicked that somebody was behind me, but there was no one there. Could she see me? Raising my hand in a final farewell, my heart hammering right up into my throat, I went back into the house.

There were sudden bangs and crashes, pops and explosions as the mob, even angrier now at the non-appearance of Seth, Ingrid, and Asa, threw bottles and lighted tapers at the tiny windows that erupted in a burst of glass, tiny sharp chips that pierced my skin, drawing blood. The old thatched roof began to smolder, tiny little tongues of heat moving amongst the straw until, with a harsh roar, bright flames of orange and gold spread rapidly, and the house began to burn, shifting and sagging at an alarming rate.

Their relentless chanting carried on and on— "Kill them, kill them, kill them—as I cowered in the tiny old kitchen of Pear Tree Cottage, smoke and ash swirling around white and airy as so many ghosts. Pulling my apron up, I held it over my mouth and nose, my breath rasping against the thin material. The metallic taste of blood lay in my mouth. And then everything began to fade, in and out, in and out and, as weak and helpless as a newborn baby, my legs slowly buckling beneath me, I began to fall.

~*~

"Chrissie, Chrissie." I felt strong, warm hands on my shoulders. "Chrissie, Chrissie, please wake up!" I felt tiny caring taps of a finger on my cheeks.

Groggily I opened my eyes. A familiar face loomed above me, shrouded in mist, which slowly, so slowly began to clear, like the sun burning away clouds on a hot summer day. I was met with a pair of piercing sea-green eyes, sexy stubble that coated cheeks and chin, and a lock of blond hair that fell enticingly onto what was, at the moment, a worried, creased forehead. Smiling, I put out my fingers and pushed the hair back into place.

"Rick? Is it really you?"

He nodded and said, "It sure is. What happened, Chrissie? Morgan Bloom? Similar to what you saw on the beach?"

I nodded and buried my head in his shoulder to hide the tears that threatened to flow at any moment. Gently picking up my hand with his, he spread it wide and slowly, seductively kissed the palm. "Oh, how I've longed for this day. I came back early. Emma has made a good recovery, and I just couldn't wait another week."

I swooned beneath his touch. But then, memories came crashing back and, with some sort of common sense taking hold, I asked him, "Did they get away?"

"Who?" he asked, his expression bewildered.

"Seth, Ingrid, and Asa Bloom—Morgan's family."

He shook his head regretfully. "I don't know, Chrissie, but don't forget what happened to them took place hundreds of years ago. All I know for sure is that I knocked and knocked on your door. I could hear you screaming and saying something about a fire. I sure was worried. I tried the door, and it opened, no problem, and I came straight in here and found you out cold."

"They must have gotten away," I murmured almost to myself. "I saw them flee into the woods—and their bodies were never found amongst the remains of the house."

"We can only hope and pray that they did eventually get to a safe place." Gently Rick squeezed my hand and then said, "Just one thing. You need to get the branches cut back on that tree of yours—it's leaning right over the garden path."

"The pear tree? Oh my God, it was a blackened stump last time I saw it!"

"Well, not anymore," he said with a grin. "It's absolutely flourishing!"

Stumbling to my feet and glancing around, I could see that there had obviously not been a fire. The house was intact and everything as it was before I went back in time and got caught up with the angry mob and the burning of Pear Tree Cottage. Rick helped me to the settee as if I was an old arthritic woman like Ingrid Bloom and then, fumbling around in the kitchen, made me coffee, black and thick, just as I liked it.

Rick stoked up the fire and, wrapped in a warm embrace, we sat watching the bright flames as they twisted and turned in the grate. We talked and talked until everything, all the worries about Lisa and Chase, his daughters and Stuart, were in the open, and there were no words left to say except "I love you," "I love you," over and over again.

"Did you speak with your brother?" I asked him.

"No, not yet. I can't—" He hesitated for a moment and said, "The time will come when I will be able to. But,"

And here he shook his head sadly, "That time isn't here yet. It cut me to the quick, Chrissie. That's why I couldn't talk about what they both did to me, even to you."

"One step at a time," I told him, in between kisses that made my lips as numb and swollen as if they'd been stung by bees. "One teeny weeny step at a time." It seemed that the fuller lip look with absolutely no surgery of any kind was mine for the taking. "Kiss me again," I demanded, and snaking my arms tighter around his neck, said, "And then again and again."

He laughed loudly, throwing back his head and showing off his neck, long and brown, a tiny pulse at the Adam's apple. His open necked shirt revealed a thick mat of curly chest hair, and this time I didn't even attempt to avert my gaze but just kept right on looking.

~*~

The shop was busy, very busy, but it was a Saturday in Whitby, and the weather was good, warm and sunny with a blue sky and a yellow sun that pulsed out heat like a living breathing thing, just as depicted on a picture drawn by a child and attached to the fridge with a magnet. The shop was a jewelers called Magpie Inc. Silver & Gold Jewelry, a high class well to do shop hidden down a windy cobbled street that simply reeked of prestige and money. Its exterior was bold and brash, the shop front windows painted deep purple and black in swirls and curls.

Necklaces, earrings, and rings winked and glittered

on sumptuous crimson, sky blue, and jade green cushions and sparkled inside tall glass cabinets just like the Crown Jewels. The floor was covered in a soft, deep carpet that covered your shoes as you sank into it.

"This place looks a bit expensive to me," I whispered to Rick as we stood patiently waiting to be served amongst all the people crowded around the counter. It seemed that everybody in Whitby was buying jewelry here today, or in the best imitation of Pete Horner I could think of, "Tom foolery—jewelry!"

"Only the best for you, Chrissie," he replied, snaking his arm around my waist and pulling me close to his warm body. "I want you to have the most beautiful engagement ring money can buy!" He stood out like a sore thumb, albeit an extremely good-looking sore thumb, his Stetson Hat perched on his silky blond head, making him appear even taller than he actually was—and, boy, was that tall!

"Blue sapphire," he said to me, leaning forward and kissing the very tip of my nose. "I can see you wearing a beautiful blue sapphire ring to match your bonnie blue eyes."

"Rhett Butler?" I asked him, and he gave me a wry smile.

Mum came into my mind and how ecstatic she'd been when I told her Rick had asked me to marry him. On bended knee and all, I'd told her. "Gawd, blimey, Chrissie, it's about time. What a hunk of a husband you've managed to get yourself. If I were twenty years younger—" Followed by the loud braying laugh. Everybody in the office—Millie, Layla, Pat, and Lily—was all over the moon, asking, "When's the wedding? Where's my invitation?" Mabel invited me around for pear wine and cake in celebration. "Trouble and strife—wife," exclaimed Pete Horner with a grin. "Yeah, I knew you'd do it one day, Chrissie Lewis, proud of you."

Gazing around, wondering how much longer we would have to wait, my heart missed a beat as a girl appeared behind the counter. She had her back to me, so I couldn't see her face. She was tall and willowy and wore a black dress cinched in with a thin belt, her waist a tiny span, and her hair rippled past her shoulders, glossy and black.

She carried a tray of rings, their stones glittering in a pool of warm sunshine. Time seemed to slow down, become languid and still, the air heavy and choking as if I were wading through syrup. A cloying, sickly syrup just like Mum's idea of a sweet black coffee. I glanced at the big round clock on the wall, its long black hands still and silent against its white face.

I reached for Rick's hand and grabbed it like a lifeline. It felt warm in mine and reassuring. He smiled down at me, sexy wrinkles appearing around his eyes, his mouth a red ripe strawberry waiting to be kissed. Slowly, slowly she began to turn, my heartbeat like a drum as I watched her. My hand in Rick's felt clammy and slippery against his skin.

"Lizzie, get a move on," said one of the other women behind the counter, nudging at the girl. "Sorry," said the woman, nodding her head towards me and Rick. "Lizzie's new here—started today." And then to the girl, she said, "Show the lady the tray of rings, why don't you, Lizzie? Yeah, that's right, the sapphire ones."

She turned fully then, and with a deep sighing breath, I could see it wasn't her—it wasn't Morgan Bloom as I'd feared it would be. I almost gave a short laugh of relief. This girl had brown eyes and a sallow complexion, and her nose was flat to her face and not tip tilted as Morgan's had been. She definitely wasn't Morgan—everything about her was wrong. Why couldn't I just accept the fact that Morgan was dead and had been for centuries, as was Seth, Ingrid, and Asa? They were all gone. It was over. All over.

My heart slowed down to its normal regular beat as we gazed at the rings, Rick picking them up and carefully placing them on my finger one after the other. Some had tiny stones set along a thin gold band, others with a larger stone, oval, round, or square, mounted on a thick band, all of a beautiful bright blue, perfectly matching my eyes. Spreading out my hand, we admired them carefully, looking at each one this way and that, to be sure of our final choice.

We'd been there for a while, as the sun had moved

in the sky and no longer fell hot and heavy across the top of the wooden counter, yet the shop was still busy, and a hubbub of voices rose all around. The clock's hands moved again, tick tock, tick tock, around its white face. I peered around cautiously for a glimpse of the girl, Lizzie, but I couldn't see her.

"What do you think, Rick?" I asked him. "Which one do you like?"

He pointed to a large oval stone of a particularly lustrous blue on a thick gold band. "This one," he replied.

"Yes," I agreed with him. "That's my favorite too." I glanced up at him, suddenly shy, suddenly realizing that this was it—we were going to be engaged and were committing to each other with this beautiful ring. I glanced back to the ring, smiling, pleased with our choice, and then, frowning, returned my gaze to Rick.

"I've never noticed that before," I said, pointing to a mole, a dark mole that grew on the soft skin just below his left eye.

He shrugged and said in his smooth Texan drawl, "It's always been there, Chrissie." And then, leaning closer to me, sexily narrowing his eyes, he said, "You've just never noticed it before."

A sudden ray of sunshine fell across his face, turning his eyes from green to yellow, a strange yellow flecked with black, like pieces of charcoal on onyx. Putting my hands to my mouth, my heart pumping hard, I gave a heartfelt gasp.

"What's wrong?" asked Rick, a small smile playing around his lips, and when I didn't reply but still stared wide-eyed, said with a frown, "Chrissie?"

Avidly searching his face, with a feeling of relief, I saw Rick, my Rick, and only my Rick, green eyes sparkling, sexy stubble coating his chin and his cheeks, his lips red and kissable. There was nobody else. What a fool I was. "Nothing," I replied with a smile, slowly shaking my head. "Nothing at all."

Even though we weren't alone but surrounded by chattering crowds, Rick took my hand, his warm fingers curling possessively around mine. Instinctively I inched nearer to him, trembling as his mouth came closer and closer still until, with an electrifying jolt, his lips met mine.

"I love you," he whispered, his breath soft in my ear.

"And you, Mr. Tex," I said, putting a hand to his notorious Stetson hat. "I love you too."

THE END

Debbie Chase (married name Debbie Spink) was born in Emsworth in Hampshire in 1959, although she has lived in West Yorkshire since 1979. She is the eldest of five children (two sisters and two brothers) and has many nieces and nephews, great-nieces and nephews, aunties, uncles and cousins, having come from a very large family. She has been married since 1984 to Howard and has one daughter, Lara, and three cats Ruby, Teddy and Maurice.

She has always been a reader and has enjoyed writing since school. Her proudest moment being when she achieved an A+ for an essay! She has had many short stories and poems for adults and children published in books and magazines. She has written four other books, the first being part fact/part fiction and called "You to Me Are Everything." The second book based on a real life pet sitting job is called "The Confessions of a Pet Sitter (from the Pet's Point of View), and the third, the sequel to that book, "What a Catastrophe (Teddy's Tale). The fourth book is a book of poems, "I Wasn't There." All four books are available to buy on Amazon and many other online bookstores as a paperback or kindle. She has also had two pocket novels ("Planning on Love" and "Romance on the Run") published with My Weekly magazine. Two more pocket novels, "Puppy Love" and "Esther Baby," will be published with My Weekly in April 2021 and August 2021. Her other novels, "Educating Maggie" and "A Step Back in Time," are published right here with World Castle Publishing, with two more "Ruby Tuesday" and "The Haunting of Pear Tree Cottage" coming out soon.

Her other hobbies are Dance Inc workouts, walking, yoga, running, kettlebell workouts and Pilates.

After many years of office work, pub work and shop work, she is now partially retired and, as well as writing, works part-time as a Dog Walker and an Examination Invigilator in a local school.

Visit her website: https://www.debbiechase.rocks/

Printed in Dunstable, United Kingdom

77913699R00122